Triple Threat

THE GALLOPING DETECTIVE
BOOK ONE

Triple Threat

CLAIRE BIRCH

A YEARLING BOOK

Published by
Dell Publishing
a division of
Bantam Doubleday Dell Publishing Group, Inc.
666 Fifth Avenue
New York, New York 10103

ISBN: 0-440-40501-7

RL: 4.3

Ages 9 to 13

Printed in the United States of America

September 1991

10 9 8 7 6 5 4 3 2 1

OPM

To Joanne Hope Birsh

Chapter One

Lucy Hill hated summer Mondays, even though she was with her best friend, Jenny, and even though she was at the Fairfax Saddlery, her second favorite place in the world. On Mondays the stable, Up and Down Farm, was closed and she couldn't ride.

The stable was definitely her favorite place, but the Saddlery was great because it was a tack shop and everything in the store had to do with horses. You could find whatever you needed to take care of a horse or to ride one. And there were all kinds of other things—horse-shaped lollipops, posters, fabulous scarfs—to take home or to buy for presents.

As Lucy arranged a bunch of riding crops in a stable bucket, her eyes went to the row of horse-show ribbons along a side wall. They were almost all championship ribbons and first-place blues won by Jenny's mother. But the ribbon Lucy looked at most was green, a sixth place in the Maclay Class Finals at the National Horse Show. To win the Maclay Finals was the highest goal for a Junior hunt-seat rider. Even to qualify was an achieve-

ment. Girls and boys under eighteen competed all year
long at horse shows around the country.

"I guess you'd settle just to make it to the National,"
Jenny said, looking up from the riding shirts she was
unpacking into a cupboard.

"Uh—sure!" Lucy said. But it wasn't true. Lucy
wanted first place in the Maclay with her name inscribed
on the trophy. She knew it was a tall order. She was
already thirteen years old. She'd never had a horse of her
own and she took lessons only in the summer. But she
was going to fix all that.

Lucy joined Jenny to help with the shirts. "What
horse did your mother ride in the Maclay?"

"Kaelie the First, a super Irish Thoroughbred. That's
why she named her new horse Kaelie II."

"Will this foal that Kaelie's carrying be Kaelie III?"

"That would be too confusing." Jenny looked toward
the stairs leading to the office. "I wish Mom would hurry.
She said only twenty minutes."

"Do we have far to drive?"

"Yes and no. The more antiques shops we have time
for, the better our chances of finding good things to
sell." Jenny cocked her ear toward the second floor. "I'll
bet one thing Mom's doing up there is arguing with the
bootmaker about Mrs. Wallace's order. The Wallace was
breathing fire on Saturday."

Jenny's slight, graceful body seemed suddenly to take
on weight and authority. Her cheerful voice deepened to
a rasp of anger. "Mrs. Lovett, I ordered those riding
boots five weeks ago. I even paid a rush charge. I want to
use them before I need a wheelchair."

Lucy broke into laughter. Jenny was thirteen, too, but

she could turn herself into a woman almost four times as old. Maybe she *would* be an actress.

Jenny slumped onto a nearby tack trunk, arms folded across her stomach. "I hate people like Mrs. Wallace who give Mom a hard time. It was different before Dad died. The shop wasn't so important and she laughed it off. But it's not just for fun anymore. The money really matters, so—"

The telephone rang and was picked up in the office. "We'll never get on the road at this rate," Jenny said.

She stared at Lucy and assumed a new pose, one hand circling in front of an eye, the other turning an invisible crank. "I am a camera," she said dramatically, "and what do I see. Lucy Hill! Star of *National Velvet III*. Her eyes are green, her face is long, her hair is too short —and that's what's wrong."

Giggling at Jenny, Lucy tugged at her brown hair. She'd been trying to grow it for a year with no luck. Still cranking one arm, Jenny zoomed in for a close-up. Tossing Lucy a smile, she said, "It's been great having you here with me every day. I wish your folks were never coming home from France."

"It's a while yet." Lucy counted the days on her fingers to hide her pleasure at Jenny's remark. "Nine more days."

Mrs. Lovett hurried down the stairs. "Sorry to have kept you waiting, girls. We're finally off." She took a deep breath. "Today's important. We'll be staying open on Mondays from now on, so this is the last treasure hunt for a while. Remember, it's the jewelry and small antiques that make us special."

Suddenly solemn, Jenny studied her mother. "It

sounds as though one of those calls was from your accountant, right? Did he tell you the July sales figures?"

"Smart girl."

Lucy felt uncomfortable. None of this was really her business. But Mrs. Lovett had been talking to Jenny about almost everything since her husband died. And during these last two weeks when Lucy had lived at their house, she'd been treated like a part of the family. Mrs. Lovett had even asked to be called Joanna.

Joanna went to her daughter and gave her a hug. She adjusted Jenny's crimped blond hair that fell from a ponytail holder.

"Yes," Joanna said, "Mr. Stewart called and the July figures are just about the same as last year. That's really bad news. So-o . . ." The word rode a long sigh. "We'll open an extra day, and we'll make a bigger effort to attract 'drop-in' customers, people who stop by just to say hello and see what's new. Most of the time they end up taking something home."

For a moment Joanna looked off into space. Then her wide smile returned. "Let's go have some fun," she said. "If we're lucky today, August could be our best month yet. Both of you look hard and see who can find the most loot."

● ● ●

By three o'clock there were a number of packages in the back of the station wagon, but Joanna had frown lines between her eyes as she drove.

"Mom, don't you like the horse-head cane Lucy found?"

"Jenny's cast-iron bank is best," Lucy said. "It's fun to watch the horse kick pennies into the slot."

"Both are fine, but we need many more things." Joanna thought a minute. "I might just keep the bank for Michael."

Lucy and Jenny nodded. Jenny's little brother had been very disappointed to be left at home.

"Carousel Antiques has always been my best bet," Joanna said. "I'm counting on them to come through again."

"Are they here in Geddings village?" Jenny asked.

"Just the other side. The shop is run by half brothers —Lee and Dean. Dean, the younger, grew up here in Geddings and at a summer house in Maine. Lee visited in July and August. When their mother died about three years ago, there wasn't much money. But she did leave them the two beautiful houses crammed with antique furniture that had belonged to the family for years. Her will said Dean and Lee should sell everything and divide the money, so—"

"—they went into the antiques business?" Jenny said.

"Exactly. Dean already had his own house here. Lee lived in Texas, but he'd just been divorced, so he moved back to Geddings and into his mother's house."

"Why didn't they just get one of those big auction places in New York to sell everything for them?" Lucy asked.

"Both men are interested in antiques. Lee studied decorative arts and you just have to hear Dean talk to know how passionate he is about beautiful things—especially clocks. In any case, the business seems to be a success."

The small village came to an end with a candy shop and a shoemaker. Bigger houses began to appear, set back from the road by long lawns.

"It's that white colonial up ahead on the left," Joanna said at last.

"That one!" Jenny's blue eyes were huge. "I didn't expect a mansion."

"The shop spreads out through most of the ground floor."

"Doesn't everything cost too much?"

"Not quite everything. Besides, Dean and Lee have always kept an eye out for things I could use at the Saddlery."

Joanna led the way through the white picket gate and up the flagstone walk. Almost at the house Jenny stopped. "Mom, look!"

At one side of the front door stood a prancing purple-and-white merry-go-round horse with a rippling blue mane and eyes so intense, he seemed ready to gallop.

"We can't leave here without it," Jenny went on. "Imagine how it would look in front of the Saddlery."

"Jenny, today we're buying items for the shop that we can sell."

"But, Mom, it would attract so much attention. I just love it."

"Jennifer, I doubt it's for sale, but we're watching our pennies, remember?"

Sometimes, Lucy thought, Jenny didn't appreciate just how good she had it, even now. When her father was alive and there'd been lots of money, she'd been allowed to have anything she wanted.

A small sign at one side of the door read CAROUSEL ANTIQUES and *Please come in.* Joanna gave the brass knocker a firm slap, then pushed the door open. Off the large entrance hall Lucy glimpsed rooms full of rich wood and gleaming metal. A tall man came hurrying toward them. He had the same dark hair and long, lean face as Lucy's father.

"Joanna! Great to see you."

Joanna offered her hand. "And you, too, Lee. This is my daughter, Jennifer, and her friend, Lucy Hill."

"How have you been all these months? Dean and I were wondering about you just the other day."

"I've been well, but my husband, Bud, died of a heart attack about a year and a half ago—just after I was here."

"Joanna, I'm so sorry! My condolences, to you and to Jenny. Somehow the news never reached us."

"I'd have been back here by now, but there were many problems with the estate and, frankly, it took me a while to get back on my feet."

She turned to Lucy and Jenny. "Why don't you explore, girls, and see what you can find for us." Joanna walked toward the doorway of one of the big rooms with Lee behind her. As she moved on, Lucy heard, "It's serious business now, Lee. . . ."

"I'm going to look in here," Lucy said, heading for a room on the opposite side of the hall.

"Sure." Jenny stared after her mother.

Wandering off, Lucy enjoyed the feeling of being alone with so many beautiful old things around her, each with a story to imagine. What sort of a family once sat around the large round table with the claw feet? Though it wasn't as fancy, the round kitchen table at home was about the same size. She looked at her watch. What were her parents doing in Paris right now? Probably eating dinner in some terrific restaurant.

Lucy quickly searched the room for horsey objects. Near the door she noticed a picture of horses and riders moving across the field in a fox hunt. The frame, made of a naturally patterned wood, was particularly beautiful.

She found Joanna and Lee in the next room, surrounded by items they'd collected.

"Joanna, look what I found," Lucy called out.

Joanna took the picture and looked it over. "This is just right, Lucy. The frame's wonderful. The picture's colorful and full of action. Lee, is this the only one?"

"Well, yes." Lee seemed to hesitate. "But I may have two more when Dean comes back. He's rushed off to an estate sale in Houston that is offering some extraordinary clocks."

"I'm sorry I missed him. Does he travel a lot?"

"Now and then. When he gets back from Texas, he'll be off to London. He buys for us there quite often and sometimes he takes a few small things to London dealers."

"Say hello to him for me," Joanna said. "Well—let's settle these prices and pack up. I'll be back soon to see what's new."

Jenny appeared from the entrance hall as Lee was saying, "I hope it will be *very* soon." There was something intense about his voice. Lucy wondered if Jenny had noticed too.

Other customers were now wandering through the house, so Joanna insisted that Lee say good-bye at the door. As they loaded the oddly shaped packages into the station wagon, Lee called from the walk, "Joanna, wait! I've got something for you."

He came striding toward them with what looked like a picture under each arm. "We have two more prints in the same frames, if you want them. All three came from a dealer upstate. Dean wanted to change the cardboard mats on these two. I just looked in the workshop and he'd finished one but not the other. If you like them the way they are, they're yours."

"Are you sure?" Joanna asked.

"Can't think of any reason why not." Lee held the pictures up for them to see. One was a hunt scene similar to the first. The other a horse and rider jumping over a big hedge.

"They're perfect," Joanna said.

When they drove off a few minutes later, Lucy was amused to notice that everyone was looking in different directions. Joanna's eyes were on the road. Lee, still standing on the walk, was gazing after Joanna. Jenny stared at the merry-go-round horse until it was out of sight.

Chapter Two

Most days when Lucy arrived at Up and Down Farm she was glad there were GO SLOW signs on the stable drive. She liked to find out who was jumping in the Main Ring at one side of the road and who was teaching in the Beginners' Ring on the other. Farther on she'd check out the horses in the paddock and see who was headed from the Main Barn to the trails or the Indoor Ring.

But this Wednesday morning was different. As Joanna drove up the dirt road, Lucy thought about her last lesson. After weeks of work Triumph had finally jumped a whole course of three-foot fences without refusing or even knocking down a rail. She could hardly wait to see if he'd "go clean" again today. The big brown horse had come from another barn for Mr. Kendrick, the stable owner, to sell. Correcting his bad habits had been her summer riding project. If she did well, Mr. Kendrick would get a better price. Maybe he would also try to find another, more advanced horse for her to ride.

"I'll pick you girls up at three-thirty," Joanna said.

"Then I can take you to the Saddlery and still get Michael to his swimming lesson."

Lucy and Jenny jumped out of the station wagon and headed for the office in the yellow farmhouse. This was the place to find out the day's lesson schedule. It was also part of the routine to say hello to Sally, who ran the office, and to Widget, the old cat who spent most of each morning in a spot of sun on Sally's desk.

Lucy studied the blackboard, grateful for the nearby fan blowing a breeze her way. "Sally!" she exclaimed. "How come my jumping lesson's moved to the morning with Erica and the Boltons? Am—am I being promoted?"

"I don't think it's that. But Mr. Kendrick wants you free this afternoon."

"He must have a reason. Can't you tell me?"

"Not now I can't." Sally turned to Jenny. "You've a private lesson with Curtain Call on the Outside Course at two o'clock. And Mr. Wilk's horse needs exercising this morning."

What could Mr. Kendrick have in mind? Certainly not exercising a private horse, the way Jenny was going to do. One of these days, Lucy said to herself, I'm going to be as good a rider as she is. Then they'll trust *me* with the private horses too. Jenny had been riding since she was eight, on her own pony, summer and winter. For the past two years she'd been working with "Curt," short for Curtain Call, a Thoroughbred her dad had given her just before he died.

Lucy had worked as hard as she could since her first lessons in the Beginners' Ring at ten. But she hadn't been able to convince her mother that winter riding wouldn't interfere with her schoolwork. And she'd never had one horse she could work with steadily until now. Triumph wouldn't be around much longer either.

Jenny started for the door. "I'm going to check on Kaelie for Mom and then clean up Curt. We can eat our sandwiches together around twelve-thirty."

"Wait up," Lucy said. "I want to see if Kaelie's bigger. I'm really having fun with this. It's the first time I've seen a mare in foal."

"Dr. Harris says she's a glutton and that pregnant mares have to watch their figures. He cut down on her feed."

Kaelie's roomy foaling stall was in the new annex at the far end of the Indoor Ring. Many of the private horses were kept there.

"Fair Kaelie," Jenny said at the stall door, "messengers arrive with greetings from Queen Joanna. Her Highness will honor you with her presence at half past three." Her voice returned to normal. "You know, she does look huge. And she's still got five months to go. I hope nothing goes wrong. Mom's really counting on selling a healthy foal."

"I never see your mom ride Kaelie anymore."

"She never has time. There's the store and Michael. And now she's trying to sell some of the artwork and antiques Dad bought for the house. You've been there when a dealer came." Jenny's face went blank and she started down the aisle. "Let's go. We've got things to do."

Lucy stayed behind to give Kaelie a farewell pat.

• • •

When Lucy brought Triumph to the Jumping Ring for her lesson, Scott Bolton and Erica, both Advanced

Intermediates, were already trotting around the ring. Steve Bolton brought his horse to the gate behind Lucy.

"Hey, Lucy Hill. How ya doin'?" Steve said. "I hear you're turning that beast into a cupcake."

Lucy blushed. Neither of the Bolton twins ever spoke to her at school. They were a year ahead of her, very handsome and very spoiled. At the stable Mr. Kendrick made everyone feel almost like a family and they usually said hello. But this was the first time she'd ever had a compliment. She put her reins in one hand and straightened her hard hat.

"So who told you that?" she said, trying to sound cool.

"Wouldn't you like to know."

Steve trotted into the ring and Lucy followed. A few minutes later Mr. Kendrick arrived, a sturdy man in his fifties, with a strong face and kind blue eyes. Along the top of his head the reddish hair had begun to thin out and turn a creamy white. He smiled a good-morning. "Let's start with figure eights at a trot. Erica first."

Mr. Kendrick's favorite word was *concentrate* and Lucy certainly had to do that with Triumph. Her first problem had been to make *him* concentrate too—to pay attention to the signals from her hands and legs. At first when the girl who owned Triumph lost interest in riding, her parents had kept the horse and let anyone get on his back. Poor riders, who didn't know the right signals, had mixed him up so badly that he'd stopped listening to anyone. Sometimes he refused to take a fence. Or he jumped carelessly, knocking down rails. Often he broke into little bucks when you'd least expect it.

Lucy still had to work at getting Triumph's attention and keeping it. But he was beginning to want to please her. Every once in a while it felt as though they were a team, as though Triumph understood what she wanted and took pleasure in working with her. His gaits might not be the smoothest, but when the two of them were moving together, when he was responsive and giving his best, it was a feeling like none she'd ever known. It usually didn't last long. That's why the previous lesson had been so special.

The jumps were set up now just like the other day— two lines of three fences each set at three feet. Scott jumped the course twice, then listened to Mr. Kendrick comment in detail. Steve was next and then it was Lucy's turn.

She cantered a circle and opened up to the first jump, but somehow Triumph wasn't set up right and took an extra small stride, then hit the fence with his front feet. She rode him hard so he wouldn't run out at the next fence, but they were both off balance at the jump. As they pounded along, she tried to get it together before the second line of fences, but pressed too hard with her legs. Triumph responded with a series of small bucks before heading into the jump. From then on Lucy felt out of control and disgusted with a sloppy ride.

She pulled up in front of Erica and the Boltons, trying not to show how awful she felt.

"Lucy, do you know what caused your problems?" Mr. Kendrick asked.

"Not exactly."

"You were looking for that clean round again. You were going for it too hard—anticipating every jump before Triumph even got there. You can't leave it to the horse to take the fence by himself. You have to ride him over it. But you can't get ahead of him either. Your legs moved back. You lost contact with his mouth. So Triumph got careless too. He didn't run out on you, but he left a lot of wood on the ground."

"Can we try the same thing again?" Lucy asked.

"Not today. We'll get to it soon enough. Take one more fence so you end on a good note. Then walk him dry."

Lucy walked circles at one end of the ring, pink with embarrassment. She'd done so badly in front of Erica and the boys! After Steve's compliment too. Then she scolded herself: Don't waste time over that. Think about everything Mr. Kendrick said. Remember how the ride felt and where it went wrong. If you want to go to the National, that's where your head has to be.

$$\bullet \bullet \bullet$$

Sitting on the grass beside Jenny, Lucy unwrapped a peanut butter-and-jelly sandwich. "It's so hot! When I came up from my lesson, I could feel perspiration making streaks through the dust on my face."

"So did Triumph behave? Another clean round?"

"Not even seven fences. I'm sort of depressed."

"Well, cheer up. I think I know what's going on this afternoon. Liz wasn't sure she'd get back from the dentist in time to teach the Beginners."

"Why didn't Sally tell that to *me*?"

"Because, silly, she didn't want you to be disappointed. But Liz still isn't here, so Mr. Kendrick's going to let you teach the class. Only a few kids show up on a day this hot, and they all trot fairly well already."

Lucy put down her sandwich. There was no way her stomach was going to be interested in food right now. To think that Mr. Kendrick would trust her with the "up and downs" was almost as great as winning her first blue ribbon. Besides, Liz taught the Beginners in exchange for her lessons. Maybe Lucy would be able to do that, too, someday.

She didn't want Jenny to see how excited she was. "I'm going to talk to Sally. I've been hoping this would happen and—" Lucy stood up. "See you," she said, and took off.

• • •

At ten minutes after two Lucy was concentrating hard on three riders, six and seven years old, moving around the ring at a trot. She tried to tune out the background noises from the houses being built on the other side of the Old Main Road.

Grace Zampkin was a solemn little girl. Lucy suspected she had much more spunk than her anxious mother ever let her show. She was beginning to post without pulling on the reins and she could keep her legs steady most of the time.

Charlie Tuthill liked to clown and just let a horse carry him around. "Charlie," Lucy shouted, "you're not on a merry-go-round horse. You're supposed to *ride* this one. That means urging him on with your legs. That means using the outside rein so that he doesn't cut corners."

Watching Kelly Stevens at the end of the line, Lucy laughed to herself. Working *too* hard wasn't good either. "Try not to post so high, Kelly. Easy up and down is just fine. Once more around the ring now, everybody. You're looking great."

Lucy was pleased. Everything had gone really well.

Perhaps she'd been a little too tough on Charlie, but he needed— Oh, *no*!

At the housing development across the road a load of lumber had fallen off a truck with a crash. Grace's horse, Sarge, had "spooked" and bolted to the side. Grace lay in a heap near the rail.

"Everyone, *stop your horses,*" Lucy shouted. "Pull back on your reins, *now.*" Fortunately, Sarge trotted only a short way and then stopped. Keeping an eye on Charlie and Kelly, Lucy went to Grace. She'd started to cry but at first glance nothing seemed to be wrong.

"Grace, does anything hurt?"

She shook her head.

"If you're sure, I'll help you stand up and we'll go get Sarge." Grace got to her feet but went on crying.

"It's a good idea to get right back on the horse. Wouldn't you like to do that?"

She shook her head.

"No?"

Grace began to sob.

Lucy wanted to insist, but the thought of Mrs. Zampkin's anxious face changed her mind. That woman would be worked up enough when she heard Grace had taken a spill.

The class had been just about over, anyway. Lucy took Grace by the hand and collected Sarge. She asked Charlie and Kelly to trot one more circle and then follow them out of the ring.

As they walked toward the stable drive, Lucy felt like crying herself. Everything had been just fine until almost the last minute. Mr. Kendrick, in the Jumping Ring across the way, would know something was wrong as soon as he saw them.

Sure enough, they'd moved only about twenty yards up the drive before Mr. Kendrick came along. Lucy spoke up before he could say a word.

"Sarge spooked, Mr. Kendrick, and Grace went off. I told her it was important to get back on the horse and asked her if she wanted to but she—"

Grace had begun to cry again. This time Lucy thought it was because she felt ashamed.

"Now, Grace," Mr. Kendrick said, walking beside them, "it's old Sarge here that should be crying, not you." His voice was kind but firm. "For ten years he's been our best horse for teaching beginners. But today he had some trouble. A loud noise took him by surprise. He moved quickly and you fell off. And if that wasn't bad enough, he knows the stable rules. If you take a spill, unless you're hurt, it's right back in the saddle."

By now Grace was looking up into Mr. Kendrick's face, turned so that she was almost walking backward. "I'll tell you what we're going to do," Mr. Kendrick went on. "When we get back to the barn, you and Lucy, Sarge and I, are going into the Indoor Ring and you're going to get back on Sarge for just a little while. You're going to do what riders are supposed to do and Sarge is going to go back to his stall feeling he's done his job right."

Later, as Grace trotted a short way in the Indoor Ring with a big smile slowly spreading across her face, Lucy looked up at Mr. Kendrick. He seemed as pleased over his success with Grace as the first time a rider jumped the advanced course without a mistake.

"That's just fine, Grace," Mr. Kendrick called out. "Now bring Sarge over to me and halt. All right, now, you flew out of the saddle last time. Let's see you dismount on your own."

Grace stammered, "Liz helps me partway."

"I see," Mr. Kendrick answered. "What do you say to that, Lucy?"

Lucy thought fast. Walking over to Grace she said, "Look, Grace, I'm right nearby. You sailed off Sarge today and weren't hurt a bit. Surely you can just slide off him now. Gather your reins in one hand and grab the front of the saddle—the pommel—the way Liz taught you."

Lucy held her breath as Grace did just what she was told. "Now swing your right foot over the saddle and . . . whoops, you got ahead of me." Grace managed to reach the ground, just barely losing her balance.

Mr. Kendrick turned toward Lucy. "You and Grace put Sarge away. I think we can count on Grace for some more good surprises from now on. You and I will talk about this again when we find a chance."

• • •

"I gave her a choice, and that was a mistake," Lucy said to Jenny when they were at the Saddlery. "I just hope he's not too disappointed in me."

"Forget it," Jenny said. "You know Mr. Kendrick better than that. He just—" She stopped as the door to the shop opened and closed. A couple in their early forties led a little girl into the store. Jenny approached them quickly. "Can I help you?" she said charmingly. It's amazing, Lucy thought. She turns into a copy of her mother.

"Heather is going to ride in the lead line class at Jarvis Farm in a few weeks," the woman said. "We'd like to buy her a riding jacket and a shirt."

Jenny led the way to the riding coats. "I think we can

see to it that Heather looks terrific." She smiled down at her. "Here is a dark navy-blue coat just like the ones the big girls wear. And it will look wonderful with this pink shirt."

The sleigh bells on the front door jangled and a tall blond man came in. He had a full face, a wavy lock of blond hair falling to one side of his forehead, and a pair of gold-rimmed glasses. His eyes roamed the shop as he asked Lucy, "Is Joanna Lovett in?"

"Not just now. But her daughter, Jenny, is helping those customers over there."

He hesitated. Then he said, "I—well, perhaps you can help me. I—I'd like to find a present for my niece who . . . is interested in horses. You can help me find something here that would be a nice present for—for her birthday."

"How old will she be?" Lucy said.

"She—she's about your age."

"Well, let's look around. There's jewelry in the glass cabinet beside the counter. Or she might like a needle-point pillow of a beautiful horse for her room. Or how about a picture for her wall? Is she a rider? Because then she might like a new pair of leather riding gloves or a colored saddle pad."

They stopped in front of a large poster of a mare and foal. The blond man said, "A picture is a fine idea. But do you have something larger and more active, like a steeplechase scene or a hunt?"

Lucy thought of the pictures from Carousel Antiques. "It's too bad. We just had three terrific pictures like that but we sold them right away."

"Well, then . . . I'll concentrate on the jewelry."

At the counter Heather played with the plastic horses

while Jenny wrote out the sales slip for her riding clothes. Meanwhile, the blond man peered into the jewelry cabinet. Finally he asked, "How much is this old necklace with the horse-head pendant?"

Jenny quoted a price, then handed Heather's mother her sales slip and left the copy on the counter. The sleigh bells jangled as a young woman came in. Lucy looked at her watch. It was almost closing time.

"I'd like to order some custom-made chaps," the woman said. That meant nine or ten measurements. Jenny told the blond man, "I need to take care of this. Why don't you think things over?"

"Thank you, I'll do that."

After a few minutes Lucy began to feel uneasy. The man was taking forever! His eyes moved from item to item, shelf to shelf. Joanna had told her that there was over five thousand dollars' worth of jewelry in that locked case. Some of the antique pieces were very rare. Lucy studied him closely.

A flock of customers arrived for little things like hoof dressing and fly repellent. Lucy wrote up the sales slips as fast as she could, trying to keep one eye on the man. Surely he could have made up his mind by now. She took all the sales slips from the counter and put them into a folder for the current week in the small file behind her.

When she looked up, he'd chosen a book from the counter display. "I'll take this now," he said. "Then I'll bring Nancy back next week and let her choose the piece she wants."

After he'd left, Lucy turned to the plastic horses that Heather had left on the counter in a heap. Each was a different breed and it was fun to arrange them. The Pinto and the Palomino looked good standing together in front.

When Jenny locked the door behind the last customer, Lucy said, "Jen, wasn't there something odd about that man? I don't think he had any niece. I think he came in to look around, and not just because he was curious."

"He didn't seem to know what he wanted, but lots of people don't."

"He hung around a very long time. He studied every piece of jewelry."

"We all know that you've got a good imagination."

"I just notice things, that's all."

There was no point in pushing it further. All she had to go on was a very strong hunch. But what if the blond man had really been "casing" the shop? Would the jewelry be a big enough haul? What else could he want?

Chapter Three

After dinner that night Lucy sat back in a lounge chair on the Lovetts' big terrace and watched Michael play croquet on the lawn beside the pool. Jenny was stretched out on a chair nearby.

"He's really a cute kid," Lucy said.

"Most of the time."

It was going to be hard for Jen and her mother to move away from this beautiful house. Joanna planned to move into a smaller place when she had a better idea of what she could afford.

But things were still pretty comfortable at the Lovetts'. Mrs. Sable came in to cook dinner most of the week and there was a cleaning woman several days. At home on a night like this Lucy would be helping to clean up after dinner, not sitting outside while a housekeeper did the dishes. Yet she liked those evenings at home when everyone was in the kitchen together. And she admired her mother, who could not only write very good documentary films but was a great cook too.

Out on the lawn, swinging his own small mallet, Michael was working his way through wicket after wicket.

Every once in a while he'd go off for a run, riding the mallet like a horse. His fine blond hair bounced as he galloped.

"You know, Jen, Michael would look even cuter in show clothes than that little girl—Heather—you dressed up this afternoon. Has he ridden at all? He may only be five, but he's better coordinated than any of the kids I taught yesterday."

"He's ridden a few times and loved it. Mom talked about starting him seriously this summer, but . . . I guess it was one more thing. I could have taught him myself, but Mom thinks you learn things better from a stranger. That's why she drags him for swimming lessons."

"He could ride your pony."

"Pirate's not my pony anymore. Mr. Kendrick has been feeding and boarding Pirate for two years and using him like a horse of his own. When Dad bought Curtain Call for me, it was a good way to keep the pony around until Michael was ready for him."

Lucy clenched her fists with excitement. "I've got an idea. Is there a lead-line class at the Rock Ridge show? Your mother will be there anyway with the Saddlery booth. You and I will be there riding in our classes. Couldn't we take Michael? I could start teaching him right away, and you could help."

Jenny sat bolt upright. "Outrageous! If he's willing to try, he can do better than lead line. We can teach him more than just walking around with someone leading his horse. But how do we break it to Mom?"

"Let's do it right now."

Joanna walked onto the flagstone terrace, coffee cup

in hand, and sat down on the flowered couch. "Isn't this a lovely evening?" she said.

"Look, Mommy, watch," Michael called, and hit a ball. "It's going straight through the wicket."

"Good, Michael. Give that ball a real whack."

Lucy tried not to stare at Joanna. She was really glamorous, but not as though she were pretending to be an actress or someone on the society pages. Just by being herself. Tonight she looked especially beautiful in white silk pants and a jade-green tunic patterned with white. Her dark hair waved around her face. She wore unusual, daring earrings. Lucy knew her own mother would think them "too much."

Jenny scraped her chair along the flagstones and Lucy looked over at her quickly. "Michael's unusually coordinated, don't you think?" Jenny said to her mother.

"Why . . . I suppose so. No more than you were at his age."

"Well, Lucy and I have an idea. Since we're going to Rock Ridge anyway and you didn't really want to leave Michael behind . . ." She gave Lucy a pointed look.

"We got the idea," Lucy jumped in, "because this afternoon a mother and father brought in a little girl about Michael's age and Jenny outfitted her from head to toe for a lead-line class at Port Jarvis—"

"Nice work, Jenny."

"Michael would look even cuter," Lucy added, "and he'd have so much fun."

"You bet!" Jenny jumped up from her chair. "Mom, we've got a great idea. Mr. Kendrick let Lucy teach the beginners' class today. She's really very good. And I could watch from the rail and help. Can't we work with Michael for the next few weeks and put him in—"

"There's no lead-line class at Rock Ridge, if that's what you're getting to."

"We haven't had time to look at the prize list. What about the Walk Trot Division? Wait!"

Jenny ran into the house and was back in seconds. She flipped through the Rock Ridge prize list quickly. "Here, Mom. There's a Walk Trot class for children under eight who haven't ridden in a recognized show. I'm sure Mr. Kendrick will let us use Pirate. When Michael's through with the clothes, we can use them for display at the shop."

Lucy could tell Joanna was considering the idea. "We're going to be working very hard Friday through Sunday at the booth. We're going to be driving seventy-five miles back and forth each day. You girls will be showing on Saturday—I've already promised you that— and you'll be helping me too. Aren't you taking on too much? You know how important that is for me. It's a trial run for selling at the really big shows . . . and aren't you forgetting something else?"

Lucy looked at Jenny, but she didn't seem to have an answer. "Uh . . . do you mean Mr. Kendrick?" Lucy said.

"Don't you need his permission here?"

Jenny moved to sit down close to her mother. She looked into her face. "Mo-om! Are you saying that if Mr. Kendrick agrees, we can do it?"

"Well—well, I suppose I am. But I'm counting on getting all the help from you girls that you promised. And, of course, we'll have to see if Michael agrees."

"Let's tell him while we put him to bed," Jenny said.

"I've let him stay up because—"

"Isn't that the front door?" Lucy said.

Joanna stood up quickly. "I'll get it."

As Joanna went into the house, Lucy looked at Jenny. Jenny raised her eyebrows, puzzled. They heard a man's voice. Then Joanna walked back out onto the terrace with Lee Cotter of Carousel Antiques.

• • •

The Lovetts' house was big enough to have extra bedrooms for guests, but Lucy and Jen had both decided it would be more fun to share the same room. For over two weeks they'd had an agreement to stop talking after midnight at the count of three in order to make sure they'd have any sleep at all. But tonight Jenny had said almost nothing from the time they'd come upstairs.

Snug in the nearby twin bed, Lucy looked over at Jenny, now lying against the pillows in a striped night-shirt and staring into space. Lucy knew why Jen was upset, but not what to say to make her feel better.

"She could at least have told me Lee was coming," Jenny said at last. "She tells me everything since Dad died."

"Maybe he just stopped by."

Jenny scowled. "Don't be silly. She didn't seem surprised at all."

"Maybe she didn't think it was important. He just stopped by for a short visit after dinner."

"So far! I could tell how much he liked her when we were at his house. So could you."

"Your mother spends almost all her time at the shop or with you and Michael. It probably feels good to have a friend around. Sometimes I think my mother doesn't really like to talk to my father. Most of the time she doesn't agree with what he says. But still I can tell she's glad he's there."

"Did you see the way he played up to Michael? And, of course, poor Michael hardly knew Daddy at all. He's just thrilled to have any man around who'll play croquet with him."

Lucy thought changing the subject might help. "It will be fun to put Michael in the horse show."

"I suppose." Jenny took a deep breath and turned on her side. "Let's just go to sleep, Lucy, okay? Or you can read."

Jenny turned off her bed lamp, and after a minute or two Lucy did the same, but she was wide awake. She'd been as surprised as Jenny when Lee arrived. After a while Joanna had asked Jenny to get Michael to bed and Lucy had gone along too. When they'd come back downstairs, Lee and Joanna were drinking coffee in the library. Lucy had talked Jenny into a moonlight swim, but she'd barely wet her suit when she was ready to quit. She'd sat at the edge of the pool while Lucy swam a few laps and then they'd come upstairs. Lee's car pulled out of the driveway soon after.

There was a picture of Jenny's father on her bookcase. He looked straight at you and Lucy was sure that sometimes Jenny must feel he was there in the room. Jenny would talk about him once in a while, but only when it was part of the conversation like "My father taught me to swim," or "Michael and I are blond like Dad." She never talked about his dying or how much she missed him.

Staring off into the darkness, Lucy thought about her own parents. They'd be home in only four more days and she couldn't wait to see them. Sometimes she'd wondered what it would be like if they got a divorce, but never about one of them dying. She couldn't even think about some new man coming along and acting like her father.

Lucy snuggled into her pillow. She'd think about the stable instead and fall off to sleep. Would they get Triumph straightened out before Rock Ridge? Why was it more important to get Grace Zampkin back on her horse than to worry about what her mother would say? As she was drifting off, she thought how lucky she was. The questions on Jenny's mind were much harder to answer.

• • •

Through layers of sleep Lucy thought she heard someone knocking on the bedroom door. She forced her eyes open and raised her head off the pillow. "Is that you, Michael?"

"It's Joanna."

Lucy sat up quickly as Joanna opened the door.

From the twin bed Jenny muttered, "What time is it? What's up, Mom?"

"I've just had a call from the security company. The police are on the way to the Saddlery and I have to meet them there."

"We've been robbed?" Jenny sat up in bed, wide awake.

"I bet it was that man," Lucy said.

"What man?" Joanna asked tensely.

"The man who was in the shop this afternoon hanging around the jewelry cabinet. He came in and asked—"

"Take us with you, Mom," Jenny interrupted. "Lucy can tell you all about it in the car. We'll get dressed in seconds."

"That's not a bad idea. Michael's been roaming around and I came to ask you to listen for him. But you girls jump into your clothes, put a sweatshirt over Michael's pajamas, and meet me in the driveway. I'll get the car."

Joanna drove quickly as she listened to Lucy's story. The police car was waiting in front of the Saddlery.

"No windows are broken," Joanna said. "I wonder if the police are inside." As she pulled the station wagon alongside the patrol car, two officers stepped out. The sergeant came to Joanna's open window.

"Hello there, Mrs. Lovett."

"What's up, Sergeant?"

"It's too bad we got the whole family out. It seems to be a false alarm. No sign of entry. No movement inside. But if you'll open up the store for us, we'll all go inside and make sure."

"How could the alarm go off by itself?" Joanna asked.

"Something may have fallen inside and activated the motion detector. Or sometimes the detector reacts to a difference in the temperature inside and out." He opened the car door for Joanna.

Lucy's stomach tightened. A false alarm would be wonderful. She certainly didn't want anything to be missing from the shop. At the same time she felt rather foolish. On the way over she'd been very definite about her suspicion that the tall blond man had come back to rob the store.

Joanna opened the Saddlery door with her key and the police entered the building. A few minutes later they threw on the lights and told Joanna to come ahead. Jenny and Lucy were right behind her, with Michael dragging on his sister's hand.

Lucy headed right for the jewelry cabinet. There was no sign of tampering and everything seemed to be in place.

Behind her Lucy could hear Joanna moving through the shop. After a while Joanna said, "At first glance everything seems to be fine. I'll check the inventory more carefully tomorrow, but it certainly seems to have been a false alarm."

"How about the cash box?" one policeman said.

"It's kept in the office upstairs. But I took the cash home this afternoon when I picked up the girls. I was going to the bank in the morning."

"Well, then, Mrs. Lovett, we might as well take off."

"I think so. I'll just lock up."

The sergeant ruffled Michael's hair and left. Michael asked for a "horse lollipop" and was choosing his favorite when Jenny came to Lucy's shoulder. "So much for your jewel thief," she said.

"I'm allowed to be wrong."

But Lucy had been scanning the shop yard by yard. As she took a last look at the counter, she felt little prickles at the back of her neck. She'd set up the plastic horses herself after Heather knocked them down. She remembered putting the Pinto next to the Palomino.

If anything was missing Joanna would know when she took inventory in the morning. But someone had definitely been in the shop after she and Jenny left. The Pinto was now in the second row. The Palomino was next to an Appaloosa.

Chapter Four

"When is Billy's mother coming?" Michael asked Lucy as they waited together at the house on Friday morning. "Billy has a beach near his house. We're going to build a castle with six towers and six tunnels."

Michael was circling the room, dropping into one chair after another with a loud plop. "Where's Jenny?"

"Getting ready to go to the stable with me. Billy's mother is giving us a lift on the way."

"Because Mommy's at the store again?"

"Yes. Give the chairs a break, Michael. Come tell me which of these horses is your favorite."

Of the many interesting things in the bookshelves and display cabinets, the best of all was the horse collection Joanna's father had started for her sixteenth birthday. There were horses of clay and glass, wood and brass, from all over the world. Several were more than two thousand years old.

Michael scurried over. He pointed to an early American toy horse made of wood. "I like the brown one with spots. My daddy bought that one. He always brought us presents when he went away." After several moments he asked, "Which horse do you like most?"

"The glass one on the second shelf. It isn't clear like most glass you see, and it has the most magical shape."

"I wish Billy would get here," Michael said, and made a run at the biggest easy chair.

Michael was more keyed up than usual, but for the past two days everyone else in the house had been too. Joanna had been organizing the merchandise for her booth at the Rock Ridge show, but she seemed distracted. Jenny was still on edge about Lee's visit, and to make matters worse she'd heard her mother talking to him on the phone several times since. As for herself, Lucy was alarmed about the Saddlery. Joanna was now certain that nothing was missing. Then what had the intruder wanted? Would he come back?

Lucy looked at Michael and went to the window again. She knew how hard it was to wait.

"Michael, I'll show you something that's fun if you promise you'll never do it without permission. You could bring the firemen and the cops by mistake."

He was at her side in a second. "Show me, Lucy, show me."

"You can play tunes by punching the buttons on a Touch-Tone telephone. On most of them, anyway. Let's try the one in the library."

Lucy punched out "Mary Had a Little Lamb" square by square. Then Michael grabbed for the phone, but she held it out of reach.

"Promise first, Michael. Cross your heart and hope to die. Never without permission. And never nine one one in a row."

"Never what?" Jenny walked into the room. "What mischief are you teaching my brother?"

Even though Jenny was smiling, Lucy felt a bit awkward. "It's a waiting game my brother Eric taught me. Michael's promised never to play with the phone without permission."

"You only know about older brothers. You can't count on these."

"One more, Lucy. Show me one more."

Lucy looked at Jenny.

"You might as well. I'd like to hear this."

Lucy was halfway through "London Bridge Is Falling Down" when Jenny saw a car pull into the driveway.

"Let's go, Michael," Lucy said. "I'll teach you the rest another time."

She was relieved to be interrupted. If Jenny didn't quite approve, Joanna might be really angry.

• • •

Lucy and Jenny peered out the car windows as they drove up the stable road. There were riders in both rings, but clumps of people—little brothers and sisters, the Bolton twins, and even parents—were fanning out around the barn and the Indoor Ring. Others seemed to be looking for something in the woods at each side of the stable.

"Let's hurry," Jenny said as they got out of the car. "Sally will tell us what's going on."

In the office Sally pointed to her desk where the cat usually sat. "Widget's missing. She didn't show up for her breakfast and she hasn't come in here. Everyone's trying to find her. She could be hurt or worse."

Jenny glanced at the lesson board. "I've still got time. I'm going out to look."

"I'll catch up with you later." She turned to Sally. "I need to talk to Mr. Kendrick. I didn't see him around yesterday."

"He was in New Jersey looking at a horse. There's someone with him now, but maybe you can get in there before his ten-thirty lesson. You'd better wait right here."

"Sure." Lucy said. "And thanks." She picked up a copy of *Practical Horseman,* but it was hard to keep her mind off Widget. She was such an old cat. A dog could have gotten to her. Or maybe she'd wandered down to the road and been hit by a car.

A faint rustling caught Lucy's ear. It sounded like a mouse. She looked on the floor beside her and below her chair. She bent down to see under Sally's desk. Finally, she went back to reading.

Minutes later she heard it again, louder. There was something different too. Could it be a faint mew? Sally was talking on the phone and couldn't possibly hear it.

Lucy stood up. Quickly she opened one file drawer and then another. In the third drawer, crumpled on top of the file folders, lay Widget. She was barely breathing.

"Sally!" Lucy yelled. "Sally. Hang up. Widget's in here!"

Together they lifted poor Widget out carefully and Sally called the vet. Lucy found Liz, who raced for her van with the cat in her arms.

When Lucy returned to the office, Sally was blinking back tears. "There's no way Widget could have ended up in the office last night. She wasn't here when I locked up. I always make sure."

Lucy had never seen Sally so upset. "I know you do, Sally. But maybe the drawer was open during the day and she jumped in. She could have folded herself up in the back so you wouldn't notice and then when you closed the drawer—"

"It couldn't have happened, Lucy. I don't think Widget can jump that high anymore. Besides, she wasn't in the office all afternoon. And what's more, I looked in that drawer about five minutes before I closed up. I needed the new blacksmith's address."

"Well, then, someone got in and out of here last night." As Lucy heard her own words, she was astonished. "Isn't that strange? That's what happened at the Fairfax Saddlery two nights ago."

"That doesn't make sense," Sally said. "Even if someone was in here, and I can't imagine what they hoped to find, how did Widget end up in the file drawer? She usually roams the barn at night or she's asleep in the tack room on her special blanket."

"Okay, let me think." Lucy went back to the wooden chair. "Suppose someone opened the door to the office and the cat came running. She could easily have pushed past someone's feet and scooted in here. Whoever was at the door would have been moving slowly. He wouldn't have known his way."

"He'd have had a flashlight."

"Even so. Anyway, you know how friendly Widget is to everyone. So, suppose this man is creeping around to find whatever he's come for and Widget keeps rubbing against his legs the way she does. She gets in his way and he loses his temper—"

"So he stuffs her in a file drawer?"

"Exactly."

"He'd be more apt to throw her across the room."

Lucy felt herself lose speed. "Uh—maybe not. Was any cash missing?"

"There wasn't any cash here."

"Well, then never mind that. Maybe this man likes animals. He just lost his patience and shoved her in the drawer."

The intercom buzzed from Mr. Kendrick's apartment, and Lucy was grateful for the interruption. "We'll talk some more," she said, and left.

Mr. Kendrick's apartment at the back of the yellow house had its own door. Lucy knocked and Mr. Kendrick called, "Come in, Lucinda." As she stepped into the room, he said, "So you want to see me. Not still worrying about that Grace Zampkin business, are you?" He motioned her to the chair by the desk. "I think I know what happened. You were worried about what her mother would say. That was a mistake. While we have these children, we have to use our best judgment. We do what we know is best for them as riders and as people. What was right the other day was to try to get the child back in the saddle."

Mr. Kendrick's pale blue eyes looked at her intently. "Now, mind you," he went on, "you have to judge your customer. Children are as different as horses. Some need firmness. Some need working around to things. . . . I guess we can call that psychology. But except in extreme cases, don't give them an out. Maintain your authority. That creates confidence."

Lucy nodded.

"I'm glad you're listening carefully," Mr. Kendrick said, "because if I guess right, in a year or two you'll have that Beginners' Ring all to yourself."

Lucy felt as though she'd just had a long drink of cold lemonade on a terribly hot day. Mr. Kendrick hadn't lost faith in her. She could hardly believe what he'd said. Now she certainly could ask him about teaching Michael.

Just then the phone rang. "Put him through, Sally," Mr. Kendrick said. Lucy gestured toward the door and asked softly, "Do you want me to go?" He shook his head.

As Mr. Kendrick talked, Lucy began to look around. The room was dusty, a sign that Mrs. Kendrick was ill again. She liked to come around and tidy things up. When she'd made her weekly visits, the couch pillows stayed puffed. It had always seemed a little silly in an office at the stable, but everyone loved Mrs. Kendrick and that was her way. Over the lumpy green couch against a side wall, Lucy was surprised to see one of the hunt scenes from Carousel Antiques. She got up to look at it.

In the crack between two of the couch pillows, there was the glint of silver against rough green fabric. Someone must have dropped some change. No—it wasn't a coin. She picked up a small pocket knife about an inch and a half long.

Behind her Mr. Kendrick hung up the phone. "I see you noticed my new picture. Nice, isn't it? Mrs. Kelly sent it to me because she's so pleased with her new horse. Embarrassed me, she did. But the thought was kind."

Lucy went back to the desk and held out the knife. "Look, Mr. Kendrick. It was between the couch pillows. I've never seen a knife this small and flat that still had so many different kinds of blades."

He examined the knife quickly and handed it back to

Lucy. "Take it to Sally, will you? Perhaps she can find the owner."

"It could have fallen out of someone's pocket," Lucy said.

"Perhaps. So, Lucy, if it wasn't Grace Zampkin, what did you want to see me about?"

"About Jenny's brother, Michael, Mr. Kendrick. Since Mrs. Lovett will have a booth at Rock Ridge and since both Jenny and I will be showing there, too, we wondered if we could try to get Michael ready for the Walk Trot Class under Eight. He could ride Pirate, and Jenny and I could work with him every day. You could come look and tell us how we're doing. Then you can decide at the last minute if he's ready, because we can enter him when we get there."

"Did you talk to Mrs. Lovett about it?"

"She left it up to you."

"Well, my only question is how much you can accomplish with Michael in less than three weeks. I assume he's interested."

"He loves the idea, Mr. Kendrick. He's very smart and very well coordinated. There's nothing to lose."

"Good, then. I'll leave it to you to work out the schedule around your own riding time. Triumph, of course, comes first."

"Of course. Thanks, Mr. Kendrick . . . for everything." She left quickly.

The screen door to the office whined shut behind Lucy as she leaned over Sally's desk.

"Sally, I'm surer than ever that someone was prowling around here last night—not only in your office but in Mr. Kendrick's too. Look what I found between two cushions on the couch."

Sally took the knife and looked it over. Then her expression changed. "I thought you had some real proof. Dozens of people sit on that couch. Mr. Kendrick talks to people buying and selling horses, to the parents of riders, grain dealers—"

"I know, Sally, but people don't usually sit on the couch. They sit opposite him on the chair near the desk." She thought a moment. "Does anyone go into the office to clean since Mrs. Kendrick's been sick?"

"Not really. I sneak in during the day sometimes and just dust the desk a little."

"Do you puff the pillows the way Mrs. Kendrick did?"

"Sometimes. But I don't want him to know I've been in there."

"Do you remember when you were in there last?"

Sally squinted behind steel-rimmed glasses and cocked her head. "About four days ago, I guess. But why would a thief be anywhere near the couch? Give it up, Lucy. There's nothing missing here in the stable office or in Mr. Kendrick's apartment either." She twisted her mouth. "I'm upset about Widget and all the time everyone spent. But it's really not that important."

Lucy straightened her shoulders. "Okay, Sally. I'll see you tomorrow. I hope Widget's feeling fine and back on your desk."

She left the office and stood in the sunlight, wondering who she could really talk to. It was too soon to get ready for her lesson, but she'd have a look at Triumph.

The big horse stretched out his head to greet her. As she rubbed the little white diamond between his nostrils, she told him about the break-in at the Saddlery and her thoughts about Widget and the knife.

"Do you believe me?" she said, stroking his face and

looking him in the eye. "Something is going on. It could mean trouble for people I care about, and they don't even know it."

Triumph tossed his head as though saying yes, but then looked at Lucy with a blank stare.

"I love you anyway," she said with a giggle. "But I'm going to get to the bottom of this, and then all of you will have to believe me!"

Chapter Five

Over the weekend Lucy had worked with Triumph on moving smoothly from one gait to another—the walk to the trot, trot to the canter, and the reverse. On Tuesday she went over it all again as they rode around the Indoor Ring. It was important to make these "transitions" smoothly by using your legs and hands in such a way that the commands could hardly be seen. As she rode against tougher competition, it would be expected.

She decided to let the horse walk for a while and then work some more. As she enjoyed the rhythm of his walk, she leaned over Triumph's neck and gave him a hug. His attitude had been great. Now, if he'd only cooperate the same way during her jumping lesson later. "Please, guy," she said patting his neck, "our classes at Rock Ridge are only eleven days away and we have to look good by then."

A horse's hooves padded behind her. Then Jennifer trotted alongside. "I watched you from the door. You two are beginning to look like a team." She brought Curtain Call back to a walk. "You might want to keep up a little more rhythm when you get back down to the walk."

"Thanks. I'll watch that. Did you just finish your lesson?"

"Yep. We're cooling off."

They walked along in silence. Since the weather was both sunny and cool, they were alone in the Indoor Ring. Jenny said suddenly, "I don't know why my mother wants to bring Lee over here."

"She wants to show him her horse. She's very proud of Kaelie."

"It's all too friendly. What does Lee know about horses, anyway?"

"Remember that first night he came to the house? Lee said he and Dean used to ride in Geddings when they were kids."

It was too bad that Jenny was so upset about something that was making her mother so happy. "Your mother certainly looked beautiful when they left for dinner last night."

"Tell me about it. I never thought she'd be like Erica's mother and go out with every man that came along."

"Jenny Lovett, you're not being fair. She's never dated until now."

"But she's only known him two weeks and she's as shiny as a trophy."

"It's not just two weeks. They've been friendly for a couple of years."

"It doesn't make sense. We're really close, Michael, Mom, and I. And my mother has lots of women friends. She loved Dad so much. It's not as if they'd been divorced."

"I don't know what to say, Jen. But . . . wait and see what happens."

Poor Jenny. It was as though she and her horse were thrashing their way out of the woods after they'd lost the trail. When that happened, branches would keep getting in the way or slapping your face when you least expected the hurt. But there was nothing to do but work your way out.

Lucy realized that Jenny was still talking. ". . . Mom and Lee will bring Michael for his lesson and stay to watch. I'm going to stand with you inside the ring, okay?"

"Of course." Lucy looked at the time. "Mr. Kendrick's working with me in fifteen minutes. Do you want to help me some more?"

"I have to put Curt away and exercise Steelman." But Jenny walked on beside her. Lucy wished she could reach over and give her a hug. Or surprise her with something that would cheer her up.

"Oh," Jenny said, "did you meet the new girl, Debby?"

"No. When did you?"

"She was talking to Sally. Her father works for some big company and they've been moved around a lot. In other countries too. Her horse is coming in a few days."

"What's she like?"

"About our age. Kind of pretty with curly black hair, cut short."

"I'll catch up with her, I guess." She gave Triumph a pat. "Look, I can't let this guy think he's finished for the day."

"I know. He can turn off like a light." Jenny sat up tall in the saddle. "Watch me. You are about to see Olympic gold medalist Joe Fargis." She urged Curt into a fast canter and rode to the door. Then she stopped her horse and tipped her hunt cap the way the International Riders do to the judging stand.

Lucy tipped her head to acknowledge the salute. Jen might never win at the Olympics like Joe Fargis with his horse Touch of Class, but she sure was a gold-medal friend.

• • •

When Lucy arrived for her lesson, she was surprised to see Scott and Steve Bolton circling the ring. She'd thought Mr. Kendrick was going to work with her alone.

"Did you and Triumph warm up, Lucy?" Mr. Kendrick called to her as she entered the ring.

"Yes."

"Fine, then. Trot once around the ring, canter a circle, and jump the first line of fences. After that come back to me."

Lucy did as she was told and Triumph jumped the three fences at three feet without any hassle. She trotted back to Mr. Kendrick. "Can I do the whole course, like the other day?"

"No. First we'll work at getting his attention, the way we've done before. Trot a small circle in front of any jump. Then pull out of it unexpectedly and take the fence. Move to another part of the ring and do the same thing. Scott and Steve, play follow-the-leader but leave plenty of space between horses."

They worked at this for a while, and Lucy felt good. Triumph was right there with her all the way. After a while Mr. Kendrick began to walk along the first line of fences, raising the top rails. Then he sent the boys to the end of the ring and raised some of the others.

"All right, Lucy. Start your circle at the canter and ask for a bit more impulsion."

Lucy started to follow Mr. Kendrick's orders, but halfway around the circle she realized that every one of those jumps was now higher than she'd ever jumped before. She didn't trust Triumph all the way. Fear brought tears to her eyes.

She trotted over to Mr. Kendrick. "Do you really think we can make those fences, Mr. Kendrick?"

"Of course, or I wouldn't ask you to jump them."

"I guess I don't trust Triumph enough."

"Are you sure? When he wants to jump, he clears the three-foot fences with at least six inches to spare. I've raised the rails only half that."

Mr. Kendrick walked over to Lucy. He looked right at her and spoke in a quiet voice. "You don't trust *yourself,* Lucy, that's the problem. You think I've overfaced you. Not at all. I've challenged you. That's what this horse needs, and so does his rider. Trust yourself and go to it."

Lucy smiled weakly and moved away. As she put Triumph back into a canter, she finally knew what it meant to "have your heart in your mouth." But when she faced the first jump she made herself concentrate fiercely. It was if she willed the horse over each jump in turn. And Triumph listened to her all the way. They only knocked down one rail at the fourth fence.

Breathless, she pulled up at the end of the ring, almost running into Scott. "Good go," he said. "Yeah" came from Steve.

Mr. Kendrick walked toward her with a broad smile.

"All right, Lucinda! Let Triumph know he's done a good job and walk him awhile."

He turned to the twins. "Boys, would you like to try this course? All right. Scott, you first."

Lucy was flying. If they were all jumping the same course, maybe she'd be promoted to the morning class after all.

As she walked out of the ring, a girl with black curls was leaning against the fence. That must be Debby. Scott and Steve had been talking to her before. She walked toward Lucy.

"Hi, I'm Debby. That was a great ride. I could see that you were nervous, but you went right to it. I'm going to be riding here soon."

Lucy brought Triumph to a halt. "Thanks. I'm Lucy Hill. You'll love it at Up and Down Farm. I've got to get a pony ready for a lesson right now, but we'll see each other again."

Lucy walked on up the drive. She leaned over and patted Triumph on the neck. Friendship was a funny thing. Debby looked like someone she would like a lot, but it took time to be real, true friends. You had to go through things together, the way she had with Jenny. If only Jenny had been down at the ring. Lucy felt two feet taller than she had that morning. When she slid off Triumph, she was almost surprised that her head came up to his neck at exactly the same place.

• • •

After Michael's lesson Lucy and Jenny rode along in the back of Lee's Jeep, while Joanna and Michael sat up front with Lee. He had promised Michael to take him to

Old MacDonald's Farm and Joanna had insisted that the girls come too.

Jenny had clammed up completely. Lucy had tried to make conversation, but finally she picked up a book she'd brought along.

"What are you reading?" Jenny said suddenly. "Is that the same book you stayed up with last night?"

Lucy nodded. "I've got to get through it. When my parents get home tomorrow, I'll bet you the first thing Mom asks is 'Have you done your summer reading assignments?' "

"Your mother gives you a hard time about school."

Lucy shrugged. "I do all right, but Mom's used to much better than that. My brother, Eric, is brilliant." Lucy was quiet a minute. "I—I think I could do better if I believed in myself more. Mr. Kendrick talked about that today during my lesson. I'm going to think about it."

Jen leaned over to see the title of Lucy's book.

"It's Sherlock Holmes," Lucy said.

"Now I know why you're seeing burglars behind every locked door."

"I just like to figure things out."

Silence returned to the backseat.

Things had gone quite well earlier in the afternoon. Joanna and Michael had taken Lee to see Kaelie while Lucy and Jenny tacked up Pirate. The lesson was fun, with Michael posting on the right diagonal most of the time. He could really tell which shoulder of the horse was moving forward and rise with the outside leg. She'd cut the lesson short because he was so excited about the trip with Lee and he'd already worked hard.

In the car the three in the front seat joked and laughed all the way. It was the same at Old MacDonald's

Farm. Lee and Joanna watched Michael dash from one discovery to the next—patting rabbits, stroking calves, following mice with his finger as they scampered through a make-believe Swiss cheese. Jenny and Lucy trailed behind. As Jenny's mood grew worse, Lucy was tempted to let her sulk and join the others. But that didn't seem fair.

"I don't see why we had to come along," Jenny said. "They could have come back for us at the stable."

"Your mom wanted everyone to be together on my last day. I thought that was—"

"Baby animals and then the ice cream parlor? She should have invited Michael's kindergarten pals."

Michael ran back to his sister and pulled on her hand. "Jenny, come. I have to show you." His face was so radiant that Jen shrugged at Lucy and went off. Lucy breathed a sigh of relief.

An hour later they were at Just Desserts, a fabulous place where you could probably buy every kind of penny candy in the world. And there were also mouth-watering cakes, giant cookies stuffed with chocolate, and ice-cream sundaes heavy with syrup and extras.

Lee took everyone's order. Lucy thought he was really quite handsome, with his dark hair and dark eyes. She liked his strong, open face. He came back to the table with a tray, piled high. Michael jumped up, hit a corner of the tray with his head, and knocked everything to the floor.

Lucy bit her lip as Michael dashed under the table. Joanna seemed to be holding her breath. Lee stood there looking down at his chinos, streaked with a rainbow of ice creams.

As a busboy came running to clean up, Lee stared at the heap of flavors on the floor. With faked seriousness he turned to Jenny. "You know, I think they forgot your pistachio." Then he sat down in his chair and reached under the table for Michael.

"Come on out here, little guy," he said. "We're all going to order again and you'll miss your turn."

Lucy thought that was neat. Would her father have reacted that way? Probably, but she'd met lots of fathers who wouldn't. As Joanna looked at Lee, her smile seemed to come from somewhere deep inside.

Jen was looking at Lee in a different way. She said, "Lee, I'll help you carry a few things this time. Then Michael won't know where to aim."

When they were finally eating, Lee asked, "Have any of you been to a hot air balloon festival? I'd really like to take you sometime. The ice cream reminded me. Before the balloons are blown up, they're lying on the field with all of the colors blending together. Then you watch them fill out with hot air and go off."

"I'd like to go in a balloon," Michael said, "but more in a tiny plane."

"I'll make a list," Lee said with a laugh.

Jenny struck a pose and began to sing softly. " 'As someday it may happen that a victim must be found, I've got a little list—I've got a little list.' "

Joanna, uncertain what Jenny was up to, began to glare.

Lee picked up the tune: " 'But it really doesn't matter whom you put upon the list, for they'd none of 'em be missed—they'd none of 'em be missed!' I guess, Jenny, you and I both had a whack at *The Mikado* in school, however many years apart."

Jenny seemed very pleased. "Our school does a Gilbert and Sullivan operetta each year. I played Yum-Yum this winter."

Joanna looked at her watch and stood up. "I've got to check my answering machine."

She came back with a message for Lucy. "A Beatrice Gaynor called."

"That's my mother's best friend," Lucy said. "She owns Perfect Pictures, the frame shop in the village."

"Why don't you run downstairs and call her back now," Joanna suggested. "She said it was urgent."

Lucy hurried to the phone. Was there some problem about her parents coming home?

Aunt Bea answered right away. "Oh, Lucy. Thanks for calling. I wanted to check about Marion's arrival. Is she still coming home tomorrow?"

"Yes. In the afternoon. You sound upset, Aunt Bea. Is something wrong?"

"I need to talk to Marion. Please tell her to call me as soon as she can. Someone must have broken into the shop. A valuable statue was stolen, but there's more to it than that. I desperately need some advice!"

Chapter Six

"It's been a pleasure to have you with us," Joanna said. She brought the station wagon to a stop in front of Lucy's house. "I'll miss you, Lucy. We all will."

The front door opened and Eric waved from the porch.

"Thanks, Mrs. Lovett. I had a great time."

There was so much more Lucy wanted to say, but Eric was coming down the walk with his big feet and long strides. He'd been away at a summer journalism program before his junior year in high school and had come home for the weekend to see their parents.

Mrs. Lovett put an arm over Lucy's shoulders. "I'm still Joanna," she said. "Come stay with us again, anytime."

Lucy opened the car door slowly. She would miss the closeness of the last weeks.

"Hi, Mrs. Lovett," Eric said at the window of the car. "What would you do if we refused to take the Mite back?" He opened the tailgate to the wagon and unloaded Lucy's suitcases.

"Keep her gladly." Joanna paused. "On second

thought, I'm not sure. That would mean you'd come to visit."

Eric grinned. But when Joanna had pulled away, Lucy exploded. "You're revolting. And don't call me Mite. Only Dad can."

"Come on, Lucy. Lighten up." Eric picked up the bags and started to walk. "We haven't seen each other all summer and we're fighting already. I wasn't going to slobber all over you in front of Mrs. Lovett, but I'm really glad to see you. Did you have a good time over there? How's Jenny?"

"I had a great time, but things are sort of difficult for Jenny and her mother."

Lucy looked around the front hall as Eric put the bags at the foot of the stairs. She walked off into the living room and took a deep breath. Home wasn't nearly as glamorous as the Lovetts', but it was a lovely place to be, filled with daylight, cheerful colors, and comfortable modern furniture.

"The folks phoned from the airport. They'll be home in about an hour. I'll bring your bags up to your room."

"I can carry them, silly."

"First-day service only. Enjoy it while it lasts."

Upstairs, Lucy sat down on her bed and looked around the room.

"No new ribbons on the lampshade?" Eric said.

"In ten days, I hope. It's my first show this summer."

"And you still swear by Mr. K?"

"I sure do. I'm riding better all the time. Ribbons aren't the only thing for riders to think about. Mr. Kendrick wants us to understand that."

Eric flopped into the easy chair in the corner. Now that he was getting older, Lucy thought, he was beginning to look like their father. For a start, they had the same black hair and blue eyes.

"So what's wrong at the Lovetts'?" Eric asked.

"Well, they miss Mr. Lovett a lot. Now Joanna's started to go out with someone. Michael thinks it's just great to have a man to play father with, but Jenny's upset. And they're worrying about money because—"

"They're worrying about money? The way they've lived!"

"I know it seems crazy when so many people are homeless and starving, but the Lovetts are used to the way they've lived. Now they have to figure out another way and get used to that. But there's something else, something strange going on that they don't even realize."

Lucy told Eric about the blond man, the burglar alarm, and the horses on the counter. She described Widget's experience in the file drawer and how she'd found the knife on Mr. Kendrick's couch. "Then yesterday," she went on, "Aunt Bea called me. She's all upset about some statue stolen from her shop. She wanted to know exactly when Mom was getting home so that she could talk to her. Eric, don't you think three break-ins in five days is unusual for Westlake?"

"I suppose. But there's no reason at all to think they're connected."

"The Saddlery and the stable could be."

"Yeah, they both have something to do with horses."

"Why is it you get away with saying 'yeah,' " Lucy snapped, "when Mom's always after me to say 'yes'?"

"One mystery at a time is enough," Eric said with a crooked smile. "Look, Luce, I don't think you've established that there *were* three break-ins."

What was it Mr. Kendrick had said during her lesson the other day? *"You've got to know when to trust yourself!"*

"Eric, I can't prove anything about Up and Down Farm. But I do know that the plastic horses fall over easily. I know I arranged them a certain way a few minutes before we locked the front door of the Saddlery for the night. Someone was in there and knocked them over. Otherwise how could they have been arranged a different way when we came in there with the police?"

"You could have remembered wrong," Eric said gently.

"I could have. But I didn't. Maybe it'll turn out there's no connection between the Saddlery, the stable, and Perfect Pictures, but I'm going to make sure. It could be important to my best friend. Maybe to Mr. Kendrick and Sally. And we don't know yet about Aunt Bea."

Eric looked at her closely. "I guess there's no reason why you can't keep your eyes open and try to figure things out. Just don't get in over your head." He stood up. "I'm going for a run. Want to come?"

"No, thanks. I'd better do a few more pages of my summer reading assignment."

"What are you reading?"

"Uh—*Pride and Prejudice*," she said. She wasn't going to give *him* a chance to tease her about Sherlock Holmes.

• • •

"I'm going to make some tea," Mrs. Hill said. "Would anyone like to join me?"

"We'll keep you company," Lucy and Eric said almost in unison. They sat down at the round table in the corner of the kitchen.

Lucy took a good look at her mother. She always

looked more serious than Joanna, that was certain. But she had a very pretty face with perfect features and nice brown eyes. Her short brown hair had grown longer while they were away. Lucy bet she'd have it cut to chin length in the next few days.

"Allan? How about you? Some tea?"

Lucy's father called from the next room. "No, thanks. I've fixed myself a vodka and tonic." A few minutes later they heard the television set.

"Your father's back at his favorite spot."

"It's his business, Mom!" Lucy said. "He needs to see the new commercials."

"Did you guys have a good time?" Eric said.

"On the whole."

Lucy tried not to look at her brother. After three weeks in Europe she'd thought her mother would be more enthusiastic than that!

Mrs. Hill brought the teapot and cups to the table. "So, Eric, is the course as good as you hoped?"

"Good enough, and I've still a week to go. Next summer I thought I'd ask Miss Gibney to let me work at the *Westlaker*. Then I'll try for a bigger paper the summer before college. We learned everything you need to do to put a newspaper to bed. It was—"

Lucy excused herself and went to the living room. She leaned over the back of her father's chair and put her arms around his chest. He reached up to grip her hand.

"Glad to see you, Mite. Did the Lovetts treat you well?"

"Of course!"

"And how are things at Kendrick's? Have you made any headway with that delinquent horse?"

"And how! His bad habits weren't his fault. Mr Kendrick says so many people were riding the clutch, his gears were stripped. He's getting tuned up again, but we're still inconsistent. And Rock Ridge is only ten days away."

"You're going for another blue ribbon?"

"Sure. I'll be showing in equitation classes, where the rider is judged, not the horse. But that isn't what's most important. It's the first time people will see Triumph in action. Mr. Kendrick wants a buyer, remember? The horse is with him to be sold."

"Right. It's coming back to me."

Lucy sat down on the floor in front of her dad. Looking up at him, she thought about Jenny. Jenny would never be able to talk to her father ever again.

"What's the matter, honey?"

"I was just thinking that Jenny can't tell her father what she's been doing . . . or what she hopes to do. . . . It suddenly hit me."

Neither one of them could think of anything to say. Finally Lucy asked, "Did *you* have a good time?"

"I think so. I did some of Mom's things and she did some of mine. It worked out quite well. And I've a few surprises for you, Mite. First of all, I dragged your mother to an international jumping competition. Quite a spectacular event. I thought I'd see what was ahead of you."

"Dad, that's fantastic."

"Of course, after watching them tear around those courses with the water jumps and all those other fiendish obstacles, I'll probably quit paying for your riding lessons in a year or so. But since you won't be ready for a Grand Prix right away, you're safe for now."

Lucy laughed. "I love you, Dad."

Mr. Hill grinned gleefully. "You're going to love me even more. I've bought you a hunt."

"What?!"

"I've bought you your own pack of hounds, Master of Foxhounds on a big reddish-brown horse—"

"A chestnut, Daddy."

"Okay, and now let's see what else did they tell me . . . Master of Foxhounds and Huntsman. You'll see—"

"A picture, Dad, is that what it is?"

"Not at all."

Just then Mrs. Hill came into the room. "Let's not keep Lucy in suspense. I'll get her present. Eric's on the phone with Jill, and that could be hours."

Moments later Lucy was pulling at the ribbon of a silver box. One by one she lifted out the most perfect painted miniatures, the metal kind like model soldiers. Her father had got it right—the hunt officials and the cutest pack of hounds in different poses. She gave both her parents fervent hugs.

Then her mother said, "And how about the summer reading assignments? Did you get to those at all?"

"Yes, I did." Lucy had to speak carefully to keep from laughing. Wait till she told Jenny. "I read one whole book and half of the other. Can we talk about them tomorrow, though? You just got home."

"I think Lucy's got a point," her father said. "Let's hold the riding talk too. Mom and I want to unpack and then we'll all go out to dinner."

"Mom—I almost forgot. Aunt Beatrice called. She's all upset and wants to talk to you about some statue that's missing from the shop."

"Did someone steal it?"

"Call her, Mom. I really don't know."

Mrs. Hill hurried to the phone in the hall. "Bea? Hello! Yes, we're fine. We had a wonderful trip. But what is Lucy telling me about some statue disappearing? Did someone break in?"

There was a long pause. "That doesn't make sense. If the sculpture is gone, someone broke into the shop or someone walked off with it right in front of you."

Mrs. Hill listened again, then cupped her hand over the phone. "Bea is saying that no one could have taken the statue while she was in the shop. It was in the work space at the back where customers never go." She spoke into the phone. "Perhaps they shut off the burglar alarm. Someone skillful could do that and deal with the lock too. Was the piece valuable? Oh, Bea!"

Mrs. Hill cupped her hand over the phone again. "It was the most valuable thing Bea's ever had at Perfect Pictures. The investigator from the insurance company seems to think she stole it herself!"

Chapter Seven

Just minutes after Perfect Pictures was due to open, Lucy parked her bike in front of the door. She walked inside and looked around. A tall woman with pale white skin and dark hair twisted in a low knot at the back of her neck strode into the front of the shop from the work space in back.

"Why, Lucy! Good morning. Is Marion parking the car? I thought she wasn't going to be here until noon."

"I came by myself. I rode my bike over." Lucy kissed Aunt Bea and said, "I wanted to talk to you, because this isn't the only place where something weird is going on."

Aunt Bea looked startled, but Lucy plunged ahead.

"It started at Mrs. Lovett's shop—you know, the Fairfax Saddlery out on the Fairmont Road."

"Were things missing there too?"

"No, but someone broke into the shop and tried to make it look as though no one had been there. That part's the same."

"Why would someone do that?"

"I've been trying to figure it out. The same thing happened at Mr. Kendrick's a few nights later."

"And nothing was missing?"

"Nothing."

"That's not the case here, Lucy. Something is definitely missing—a beautiful figure of a woman from Tanagra in ancient Greece. That's why I'm in trouble." Aunt Bea clasped her hands. Her shoulders rose and fell with a deep sigh.

"I know, but I'm beginning to think someone is breaking into these places to find a particular thing and they don't want people to know they've been looking. At the Saddlery everyone thought the burglar alarm went off by mistake. At the stable there wasn't any real proof of a break-in either."

"Lucy, I love you very much and I appreciate that you're trying to help. But this is nonsense. Whoever came here took the most valuable thing in the place and left me in a terrible spot. Darling, I'd better get back to work if I'm going to take off time to have lunch with your mother." She started toward the back of the shop.

Lucy followed. "Aunt Bea, whoever came in here turned off the burglar alarm. It was supposed to look as though no one had been here. That part's the same."

"What burglar would want the alarm to go off here? Perfect Pictures is in the center of Westlake village with the police station four blocks away."

Lucy stopped in her tracks. "I—I see what you mean." She looked around, trying to hide her confusion. There was a large worktable against the back wall. At one side framed pictures stood in wooden racks. Aunt Bea opened a large closet on the opposite wall where there were more racks under a number of shelves. The pictures in these racks were matted but not yet framed.

"This is where the Grecian lady was standing," Aunt

Bea said. "Right over here." She rubbed the shelf with her hand. "I was supposed to design a special base."

Lucy studied the closet. Wait a minute. The plastic horses had fallen over at the Saddlery. The intruder had probably been working with a flashlight in the dark. Lucy looked toward the front of the shop. He'd certainly have used a flashlight here. He'd never have turned on the lights in a store that was in the center of the village with glass windows across the front.

"Aunt Bea, please do me a favor. Could we take the pictures out of the bottom part of the cabinet here? I'll do it myself and promise to put them back carefully."

Aunt Bea was starting to become annoyed. Lucy tried not to notice.

"Please, Aunt Bea. I've got a very good reason. If I'm wrong, I'll leave right away. If I'm not, you'll understand."

"Oh, all right. I've known you since you were in diapers. I'll humor you here. But then out. I really have to work."

"What was the statue made of?" Lucy asked, as they removed the pictures from the closet together.

"Tanagra was a part of Greece known for figures made of unglazed clay. This piece was a pinkish tan."

Lucy knelt down as the last pictures came out of the closet. She looked hard at each pair of wooden slats. It was difficult to see without more light. Finally she rubbed her fingers along the floor.

"I imagine you'll find some dust down there," Bea said, "though I try to keep after it."

Lucy raised her hand to the brighter light and studied her fingertips. Her hand tensed. "I don't think this looks like ordinary dust."

Bea bent to look at her hand. "Wait. I'll get a flashlight."

When she came back, Lucy held the light over the racks. "Look! There's a fine pinkish dust here. And even a few tiny pieces back here. I was right!"

Lucy stood up. "I think the statue was broken while they were hunting for something else. If they'd left the pieces, you could have shown them to the police as proof that there *had* been a break-in."

Aunt Bea nodded slowly. "At worst the police and the insurance adjuster would have thought I was the one who broke it." She sat down on a nearby stool. "I don't know what to make of this. I think you're right, Lucy, but unfortunately, no one will believe a word of it."

"They will if you leave the dust there."

"I don't think so. What were they looking for?"

"Something else they thought might be in the shop. And I guess it had to be a picture, if they were looking through those racks." Lucy's mind began to race. If the break-ins were connected, maybe they were looking for a picture at the stable too. And the only—

Aunt Bea shook herself. "I'm going to work." She carried a matted print to the workbench. "I'm usually weeks behind on orders, but I promised to do a new mat on this picture for Laura Wallace's birthday. Her mother is one of my best customers."

Lucy rushed to look. "It's a picture from the Saddlery. I was with Mrs. Lovett when she bought it. Mr. Kendrick has one too. That could be the connection, Aunt Bea! It could. I have to think a minute."

The connection between the stable and the frame shop must be two prints. They both came from the Saddlery. But how would anyone know where they were?

One was a present to Mr. Kendrick from Mrs. Kelly. The other had been bought by Mrs. Wallace and sent to Perfect Pictures.

"Aunt Bea, did Mrs. Wallace bring the print in herself?"

"No, she sent it directly from the Saddlery. Then a few days later she brought in a snip of fabric from Laura's bedspread."

Of course! Lucy felt as though she'd taken the last fence in the Show Ring and "gone clean." Now she understood the break-in at the Saddlery too. All the pieces fit together. When the blond man first came in, he'd studied everything in the shop. He'd been looking for the pictures. Then she'd told him about the Carousel Antiques pictures and how they'd been sold in just a few days. After that he'd gone to the jewelry.

"Lucy," Aunt Bea said, "don't leave me in suspense."

"I won't." But she continued to think. He'd looked at the jewelry for the longest time. That's why she'd been suspicious. But the jewelry cabinet was right next to the counter. If he'd come looking for the pictures and found them gone, wouldn't he have thought about how to find them? That would have meant looking for the sales slips. She'd only taken her eyes off him once to put a packet of sales slips into the file cabinet. When she'd turned around again, he'd been holding that book in his hand, ready to go.

At the worktable Lucy reached up and kissed Bea's cheek. "I've got to get over to the Saddlery. If I'm on the right track, your problem may disappear."

Aunt Bea smiled. "I can't wait to tell Marion what a very special girl she has."

Lucy's face fell. She hadn't told her mother she was

stopping off at Perfect Pictures. Her mother would think she was getting herself involved in things that were none of her business. But she had no time to worry about that now.

"Uh—could you tell Mom as little about my visit as possible? And thanks for your patience, Aunt Bea." Lucy headed for the door.

"Do keep me posted," Aunt Bea called after her.

"Of course!"

Lucy hurried to her bike and bent down to remove the lock. For the first time in her life she wished she could shift her riding lesson. But there was her lesson and Michael's too. After that she'd leave her bike at the stable and go back to the Saddlery with Jenny the way she'd done these past weeks.

You have to get into those sales slips, Lucy said to herself. If you're right, two will be missing. No, not two. *Three!* She'd lost sight of the third picture altogether. The burglar had left the first two pictures where they were. So it was the third picture that he was after. Who had bought it? What would happen when the thief tried to get it?

She hadn't made it "clean" to the last jump at all. This mystery was far from over.

Chapter Eight

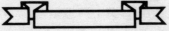

The bike ride from Perfect Pictures to the stable was a long stretch. Lucy had time to think about how to get into the file behind the Saddlery counter without explaining to Jenny what she was trying to find. After a while she decided it was silly to pretend. Jenny liked to tease, but they were still best friends.

It had been good to be home last night, in her own room with her special things—the champagne bottle from her grandparents' fortieth anniversary, the poster advertising the National Horse Show, the ribbons on her lampshade—however few. And yet she missed being at the Lovetts'. The way Joanna went about things was terrific, with her big smiles and her easy manner. Like taking Michael along the other night in his pajamas. And the way she trusted Jenny and Lucy to look after the Saddlery.

The best thing about Lucy's own parents was that they were hers. She could count on them, each in different ways, and on Eric too. "People are as different as horses," Mr. Kendrick always said. Well, the reasons she loved Triumph and Kaelie and Moonrock—Mr. Kendrick's own hunter—couldn't be measured one against the other. Her family and the Lovetts were something like that.

Lucy raised her hand in a mock salute to the horse's head on the stable sign. As she pedaled up the dusty stable drive, Domino, the stable Dalmatian, came running. "Too bad Mr. Kendrick takes you home at night," Lucy said. "Otherwise you'd have barked and Freddie would have heard you in his room above the stable. Maybe he'd have seen that burglar."

In the parking area Lucy slid her bike into the rack near the office and walked into the main barn. The stable smell wasn't for everyone, but Lucy loved the combination of hay and wood-shavings, leather and liniments. At Up and Down Farm every impression was underlined. She knew the exact pitch of the whine in the screen door to the office. She knew the length of the shadows from the jumps in the Main Ring in the afternoon. She felt more alive here than anywhere else.

Lucy slid on Triumph's halter and brought him to the crossties in the aisle. She'd find Jenny and talk about the sales slips later. Right now she welcomed the familiar rhythm of brushing the horse and the faint scratching sound. She felt the familiar contours of his neck and shoulders under her hand and resolved again that she was going to become the best rider she could possibly be. Every hour on horseback had to count, every lesson and every horse show. Rock Ridge was only eight days away.

• • •

Later that afternoon Lucy sat behind the counter at the Saddlery enjoying a frozen yogurt. Jenny was straddling the wooden saddlehorse in the middle of the store, but Lucy had made sure to get close to the small file.

"Michael's beginning to look good," Lucy said. "He's a natural on a horse, like the rest of you Lovetts."

"It's odd to see him on my old pony. But I like it. Mom was fitting him yesterday with the cutest little pair of paddock boots. I think she's excited about this too."

"I hope Mr. Kendrick will think he's ready."

"He will. So, why did you wait till today to tell me that the horses on the counter were moved around? All you had to say was 'Jenny, there's a crazed maniac around who rearranges plastic horses, puts cats in drawers, and leaves trinkets between pillows.'"

Lucy could feel the top of her ears getting warm. "Ha, Ha, Jen. You're funny, but . . ." Her words petered out. She picked up one of the riding crops from the bucket nearby and pulled at the leather thong.

"Loo-cee," Jenny protested. "You're my best friend. You should know when I'm clowning around. When you asked to come over, I hoped you were just lonesome after two days away from my wonderful presence. But alas, you said it was the sales receipts that were bringing you here, so take a look."

Lucy turned around to the file drawer and pulled out the folder with the August sales slips. As she put it on the counter, she was pleased to hear the jangle of sleigh bells on the door. A customer meant that Jenny wouldn't be looking over her shoulder.

The slips from each date were in rubber bands, so it was easy to make her way back to the day at Carousel Antiques. Was it only eleven days ago? No wonder Jenny thought things had been moving quickly between Lee and Joanna. Lucy remembered how Lee had come running down the path with the two other pictures. Surely, he hadn't known of a problem. But whoever sold the pictures to Lee and Dean in the first place might have discovered their mistake.

Lucy isolated three piles of sales slips. All three pictures had been sold at the Saddlery within three days. Beginning to breathe faster, she removed the rubber band on the first day's pile. She turned over one slip after the next, careful to keep them in order. At the back of the shop, in the make-believe box stall, Jenny was going on about nylon versus leather halters. That was just fine.

Lucy caught her breath. It shouldn't be there, but it was! Mrs. Kelly's sales slip with the instruction: *Deliver to Mr. John Kendrick at Up and Down Farm.* She banged a fist on the counter. Did this mean she was wrong?

Maybe not. She'd assumed that once the burglar found the sales slips, he'd have grabbed them and taken off. The burglar alarm was ringing. The police would be coming. But Up and Down Farm was an easy name to remember and so was the address—Old Main Road. She put the first batch of slips back together inside the rubber band and picked up the second pack.

Again Lucy turned over one small yellow piece of paper after another. About halfway through the pile she began to hope. Slip by slip her excitement grew. Then with only two left, she sat down on the stool behind the counter with a thud. There it was—Mrs. Wallace's name and the address of Perfect Pictures.

Well, Perfect Pictures was an easy name to remember too. Or maybe the thief had just copied down the names on a piece of paper. Why hadn't she thought of that? Or had Lucy Hill played the old connect-the-numbers game all wrong? Maybe she'd just hooked up a lot of dots into the shape she wanted to see, and not the real picture at all?

"How're you making out?" Jenny called.

"I'm still at it."

Lucy turned back to the last stack of receipts. This time she had to read more carefully because she had no idea of the purchaser's name. She looked for a yellow slip with the word *picture* or *print,* but none was there. She straightened the stack of slips and began a second time. As she went along, her mind charged ahead. The thief wanted it to look as though no one had been there. Each stack of slips had to be opened and handled carefully. It all took time. Maybe by stack three, time was about to run out. Maybe he grabbed the third slip and ran. Until the end of the month no one would have noticed it was missing.

Jenny brought her customer to the front counter and took care of the purchase. When the young man left, Lucy said quickly, "Do you know who bought the third picture?"

"No. I never asked."

"We've got to find out. Could we talk to your mother real soon? She'll know, and she can decide whether to warn them or not."

"Warn them?"

"Yes, Jen. They're going to be robbed."

● ● ●

Mrs. Hill wasn't happy that Lucy wanted to stay overnight at the Lovetts' "the day after Dad and I came home," but she'd finally agreed. The house was a long way from the Saddlery, but since Joanna had an appointment with an art dealer, Lucy and Jenny decided to bike it. Lucy's legs began to ache, but the thought of the third picture kept her going.

When they arrived, Joanna was alone in the living room. "I'm delighted to see you back so soon," she said to Lucy, "but what is this all-important question you need to ask me?"

"It's about the third picture from Carousel Antiques. I know Mrs. Kelly and Mrs. Wallace bought two of the prints, but there doesn't seem to be a sales slip for the third."

Joanna clapped a hand to her forehead. "I took that print myself and forgot to put in a slip." She blushed and said, "I guess my head's been in the clouds lately."

Lucy tried to collect her thoughts. For a moment Jenny looked disgusted, but she wiped the expression off her face. "So is the picture here in the house, Mom?"

"No, I gave it to Mr. Shields." Joanna turned to Lucy. "He's my lawyer and he's been an enormous help to me since Bud died. His six-year-old son is riding now, and I thought it would make a nice present for the boy's room."

Joanna looked at the girls closely. "What's the matter with you two?"

Jenny made one of her dramatic faces. "It's your story, Lucy."

"Mrs. Lovett," Lucy jumped in, "you remember the call from Beatrice Gaynor, my mother's best friend? I went to see her today because something odd happened. There was a valuable Greek statue in her shop and it disappeared during the night."

"Someone took it?"

"Yes, but I don't think that was the plan in the beginning. I think the thief broke the statue by mistake and took the pieces away so there wouldn't be any evidence of a break-in."

"See, Mom, Lucy's sure someone broke into the Saddlery too. She insists she remembers exactly how she left the plastic horses and that they weren't the same when we got there. She thinks someone broke into the office at Up and Down Farm and into the apartment too."

"Girls. You've lost me."

Lucy stammered, "I think I finally know what's behind all this. It's those pictures from Carousel Antiques."

"Lee's place!" Joanna shook her head.

Lucy rushed on. "Here's the point. Mr. Kendrick has one of the pictures. There was a break-in at the stable, but nothing was taken. Beatrice had one of the pictures in her shop. It wasn't taken either. You remember that suspicious blond man I thought had robbed the store the night we all drove down there. I think he came about the pictures. The first thing he did was ask for you. Maybe he was going to try to buy them back. Anyway, I told him these great pictures full of action had already been sold. So, he knew they weren't in the shop anymore. He must have come back that night to look through the sales slips. He certainly hung around the counter long enough to see where we put them—"

"The point is, Mom, neither of the other pictures was the one he wanted. That means yours is."

Lucy rushed on. "I've been reading some Sherlock Holmes stories for my summer reading assignment and there's this story called 'The Adventure of the Six Napoleons'—"

Joanna stopped her. "Perhaps the picture I took is

particularly valuable. The dealer who sold it to Lee and Dean may have found out later."

"Well, maybe. Or I've another idea. The 'Six Napoleons' is about a stolen pearl that was hidden in a plaster statue of Napoleon by the thief. He'd been chased to the factory where he worked, and stashed it in one of six statues that were all alike. Much later he got out of prison, looked into who'd bought the statues, and checked them out one by one. Of course, there was some murder along the way."

Lucy went on, "Maybe something really valuable was hidden inside one of those frames and the picture was sold to Carousel Antiques by mistake."

"Lucy, this is all very creative and I admit you've set me thinking. But the picture isn't here. What is it you want me to do?"

"Could you call your lawyer and ask him to open the back of the picture you sent—just to see if anything is hidden there?"

"My goodness, that would be a nuisance for him."

"Please, Mom. I didn't believe Lucy and I've teased her plenty. But she's convinced me. At least find out if there's anything to this. If there is, you can go to the police."

Joanna reached up and pulled off one earring. She rubbed her earlobe and put it back.

Jenny chuckled. "Mom's thinking about it. That's the sign."

"You're right, but I don't see how I can bother Mr. Shields with so little to go on. I think you've been ingenious, Lucy. You've put a number of pieces together so that they appear to fit, but they can all be explained some other way. Like the missing sales slip. There was a simple explanation. I didn't make one out. And what if your memory about the horses is wrong? Then the burglar alarm may really have gone off by itself. And what proof is there of a break-in at the stable?"

Lucy decided to skip the part about Widget. "There was a little silver knife on a couch where no one ever sits. I've been thinking about it some more. The picture you took and the picture Mr. Kendrick has are the two hunt scenes. They look a lot alike. Mr. Kendrick's picture is hanging over that green couch. If someone came in there with a flashlight they probably had to kneel on the couch to make sure which picture they were looking at. Then maybe they took something out of their pocket, like a handkerchief to wipe the glass, or a tool to fix the lock again, and maybe the little knife—"

"Lucy, Lucy, I had no idea you were so imaginative."

Jenny's head was moving up and down in an exaggerated way like a nodding horse. "She's *that,* all right."

For a minute Lucy thought it might be rude to keep arguing. Her mother would certainly say so. But something made her go on.

"There's one thing more. I think whoever is after this picture hoped the break-ins would never be connected. I think he hoped to get in and out without anyone knowing. When he found the right picture he'd have taken a lot of other things so no one would know what he'd come for."

"Why do you say that?"

"Because once all this was hooked up to the pictures it could be traced right back to Dean and Lee and from them to the place the pictures came from."

"Girls. I adore you both, but I've had enough of this for one night. I promise to think it over. Just possibly, I'll phone Mr. Shields tomorrow at his office. To call him at home would be— Excuse me. I'd better get that." She went to the phone.

Jenny looked at Lucy. "Good try. You have to understand that—" She stopped.

"Who is this?" Joanna's voice rose. "Why are you calling *me*?" Lucy held her breath. Jenny stared at her mother.

Joanna listened. "Don't threaten me. I don't have the picture and I can't get it." She listened a minute longer, then slowly put down the phone.

Chapter Nine

"**M**om! Are you all right? Who was that?" Jenny stared at her mother.

At first Lucy thought Joanna might faint. Even the suntan seemed to have drained from her face. She stood absolutely still, as though trying to catch her balance. Then she said quietly, "How dare that man? What made him think I had the picture anyway?"

"What exactly did he say?" Lucy asked.

"What was his voice like, Mom?"

". . . A-a . . . rather gruff voice . . . a strong voice used to giving orders."

"But no one you recognized?"

"No, Lucy. Not at all." Joanna walked to a nearby chair and sank into the pillows. "Well, Miss Hill, I guess you were right that there's a mystery connected with the Carousel pictures. That man certainly wants one of them back."

"What did you mean, Mom, when you said 'Don't threaten me'? What did he say he would do?"

Joanna stared into space and closed her eyes for a second. "It's hard to believe I'm talking about something that actually happened. He said he knew that the Saddlery had bought three pictures in matching frames. He knew where two of them were but not the third. He said that, of course, I knew where the third one was and that I was to get it back and he would phone with further instructions in the next few days." As she took a deep breath she seemed to shake.

"Mom! I can't believe this," Jenny said.

"Neither can I."

Lucy had trouble finding her voice. "But what about the threat, Joanna?" she managed to say.

"That man said in the ugliest tone, 'Don't kid yourself, lady. This is serious business. And I'll make sure that you know it.' Then he warned me not to go to the police." She closed her eyes again and lay back against the couch.

Neither Lucy nor Jenny said a word. It was as though what they'd heard might not be true if they refused to acknowledge it. Suddenly Joanna sat up straight, shook her shoulders, and said in her strongest voice, "This is ridiculous. What good would it do to go to the police? They won't act on a single, unverified phone call. And certainly all this business about break-ins with nothing missing would make as little sense to them as it did to me." She paused to think. "I'll set my answering machines here and at the office to record conversations as well as messages. If this whole thing is more than nonsense, I'll have proof next time. I don't see what else I can do. I've got to keep my mind on the Rock Ridge show. Making a success of that booth is important to me."

Jenny sat down next to her mother on the couch. "I think you should tell Lee what's happened and let him deal with it. After all, the pictures came from him. He knows where he and Dean got them. He may even know the reason why these people . . ." She stopped herself there.

Lucy spoke quickly. "Now you can certainly call your lawyer. Could you ask him to take the picture apart? Or could you go there and do it for him? If something really is hidden in the frame, you'll have evidence to take to the police."

Joanna's face brightened. "Good thinking, Lucy. My brain isn't working. I should phone right now."

For a moment Joanna handled the receiver as if it were an unfriendly reptile. But she punched out the number and Lucy waited eagerly.

"I'm not getting an answer." Joanna held the phone to her ear a moment longer, then suddenly dropped it to her lap. "How stupid of me. When I brought the picture to Frank he said he was leaving in a few days to take his family to Europe. Of course. They're away." She listened again, then hung up.

Lucy had never seen Joanna so solemn. "I'll call Frank's office in the morning," she said. "But I think I'm out of luck."

$$\bullet \ \bullet \ \bullet$$

The next morning it was hard for Lucy to believe the telephone call had really happened. Joanna, it turned out, had been right that her lawyer was in Europe. To make things worse, he was traveling by car and checking with his office only once or twice a week.

Now that Lucy knew she'd been on the right track about the break-ins, she was concentrating on who wanted the picture so badly. Was it the blond man? Was he working for someone else? She wondered, too, if Joanna had told Lee about the phone call yet. Shouldn't Joanna be taking the threat more seriously?

But Rock Ridge was only a week away. Joanna, with Lucy and Jenny's help, was trying to finish everything she needed for the Saddlery display—the furnishings for the booth, the merchandise inventory, and the price tags. Lucy was preoccupied with extra hours on Triumph and Michael's daily lesson. Jenny was working hard with Curt.

The weather, too, was diverting. The sky was an endless blue blanket with a few puffs of white lint. It was hard to fit anything disturbing into this sunny picture.

• • •

Saturday afternoon, Kaelie walked into a nest of hornets out in the pasture. Since the medicine usually prescribed for hornet stings would hurt her foal, Dr. Harris said all they could do was to keep her comfortable and check every four hours for signs of shock. Freddie, the groom, was getting out of bed at two A.M. and at six, so Joanna had taken on the ten P.M. barn visit. Lucy offered to do it for her on Sunday night because Jenny's grandmother had come to visit.

"Thanks, Mom. I appreciate the lift," Lucy said as her mother drove into the parking lot at Up and Down Farm.

Mrs. Hill stopped the car as close to the Indoor Ring as she could get. Up and Down Farm looked very different at night. There was one big light on the drive and another in the parking lot. The bug zappers gave off clouds of eerie bluish light and the moonlight cast unexpected shadows.

"I don't mind at all, Lucy. It's the least we could do after the Lovetts let you live with them for almost a month." After a moment Mrs. Hill said, "I suppose Jenny misses her father very much."

"She won't talk about it. Right now she's upset because her mother's beginning to like someone quite a lot. They go out to dinner, and he comes over to the house. Jenny doesn't want anyone else to act like her father. She hates Lee, and he's actually a very nice man."

Lucy was in no hurry to get out of the car. It was nice to sit with her mother at her favorite place with the moon shining down on them and no one else around.

Mrs. Hill was thoughtful. Then she said, "I worked on a movie once about stepparents and stepchildren. I think you were too young to remember that one. I talked to the experts and read a great deal, as usual. It seems that resistance to a stepparent isn't always just love for the natural parent. Sometimes it's because children like having the surviving parent all to themselves. Jenny may not want to share her mother. Her own father was one thing. But a new person is another."

"Mom, you're so smart!" This was something to think about.

Mrs. Hill reached for Lucy's shoulders and gave her a hug. "Well, thank you. Now run and take care of Kaelie so we can get back home."

Lucy slid out of the car. "I won't be long."

She walked along the path beside the long Indoor Ring to the extra stalls built at the back end. The barns were never locked. The stable had been here so long, it had probably never occurred to Mr. Kendrick that anyone would steal a horse. But it had to do with fire too. Freddie said you had to get the horses out fast.

Lucy pushed the front door open and reached for the light switch. Her hand stopped halfway. The barn sounds were unnatural for this time of night. She flattened herself against the nearest stall and listened. The horses were too keyed up. They were moving around as though they knew they were going to eat.

Lucy saw the beam of a flashlight from the feed room at the far end of the long aisle. Her heart began to pound. And now she heard a deep voice muttering. She inched along the stall to a small jog in the supporting wall that would give her a place to hide. Pressing back as far as she could, she forced herself to think. Should she make a run for it? She was close enough to the door to dash for her mother's car. They could wake up Freddie, who would be in his room above the Main Barn.

No. She could do that when she'd found out what was going on. Whoever was in the feed room didn't belong here. Otherwise he'd have flicked on the light switch. Some horse might be in danger. Could this be connected to the phone call to Joanna? Lucy's stomach seemed to drop to her knees as she realized which horse it must be.

Suppose the man had come to kill Kaelie. He'd have a gun. Or what if he was just going to steal her? Then the sooner someone called the police, the better. She'd made a mistake. She'd better get out of here fast.

The beam of light rounded the doorjamb of the feed room and flared up the aisle. It was too late. Lucy sucked in her stomach and prayed that the man wouldn't see her. She thought of one piece of luck. Kaelie's stall, if that's where he was heading, was a good distance up the aisle from where she was hiding. The spill from his flash might not reach her.

Footsteps, thudding against the cement aisle, came

closer. Moonlight through the back door outlined the large man's work clothes and the bucket he was carrying. As he moved down the aisle, Steelman stuck his head out of his stall and the man moved away fast.

Lucy could hear the feed rattling in the bucket. The feed must be poisoned. All he had to do was drop it into Kaelie's feed tub through the open hole in the stall. That glutton would bolt it down.

Fear for Kaelie overcame Lucy's fear for herself. *Think,* she told herself, *think.* She'd have to wait until he gave Kaelie the poisoned feed. It would be a mistake to make a move until his back was turned. But then what?

The man moved down the aisle past Galileo, past Moonrock, past Copper Penny. Stop, now, please! Stop at the next stall. That's Kaelie. You know that already. Stop th— He did. And now a plan had jumped into Lucy's head.

This man didn't seem so comfortable with horses. He'd ducked pretty fast when Steelman stuck his head into the aisle. Robocop was in the stall behind Lucy. He was a big rangy hunter who loved to get out of the barn. She tensed her body and clucked to him softly. He came right to the door.

The man stopped in his tracks. Lucy clenched her fists. He moved on to Kaelie and emptied the bucket.

Now there was no time to lose. The man hurried up the aisle, heading for the back door toward the woods. He turned off his flash, relying on the moonlight ahead. Moving as quickly as she could, Lucy opened Robo's stall and, with a whack on the rump, sent the large animal clattering down the dark aisle after the man. Quickly Lucy jumped across the aisle to Caesar and let him loose too.

Was the man coming back toward her? The horses blocked her view and there was no way to hear his footsteps under the sound of their hooves. For now, the animals formed a barricade. Lucy dashed for Kaelie and grabbed the halter beside her stall. Yanking her head away from the food, she slipped the halter on as fast as she could.

"Come on, girl," Lucy said softly, pulling her out of the stall. "Come out of here fast."

The sweet-tempered mare followed Lucy to the door. Lucy hoped she'd guessed right and the man would close the back door between himself and the two loose horses. If not, Robo and Caesar might take off into the woods. What if he let them run out and started back after her? He certainly wouldn't want a witness. The only thing she could do was keep moving.

Outside the barn she hurried Kaelie along the path toward the car. "Mom," she shouted. "Help! Lean on the horn. There was a man in the barn after Kaelie."

The harsh blare of the horn split the nighttime quiet.

"That'll bring Freddie," Lucy said to her mother at the car. "Quick. Hold her. I have to find Robo and Caesar."

"Lucy, slow down. Tell me what happened. Shall I call the police?"

"Hey, what's up out there?" a voice yelled across the parking lot.

"Saved," Lucy said, feeling weak at the knees. "Freddie, it's Lucy. Come quick."

He ran up to her, half the buttons open on his shirt. "Someone tried to poison Kaelie," Lucy said. "I got to her before she could eat much, but we need Dr. Harris.

Oh, but first we should see if he shut the back door. Otherwise Caesar and Robo are out there loose. . . ."

"What are you blathering about, Lucy?" Freddie took Kaelie's lead and started back toward the barn. "Come along. You can tell me while we put the horses away. Mrs. Hill, there's a pay phone near the door of the big barn. Please call the police."

For a moment Lucy couldn't move. What would Jenny and Joanna think of all this? That man with the gruff voice on the telephone had said he meant business. He'd shown them. But he hadn't pulled it off. It seemed as though she was taking the first deep breath of her life.

Mrs. Hill turned to Lucy. "Are you all right?"

"Yes, Mom. Really." She stood up tall. "Meet you back here."

There was something new about the way her mother was looking at her. Lucy liked it a lot.

Chapter Ten

Early Wednesday morning Lucy lay in bed thinking. It was much scarier to wonder about what would happen next than to do your best with what was in front of you.

And she *had* done her best. With lots of trouble to show for it. The last two days had been much tougher than the ten minutes of danger in the barn on Sunday.

First thing Monday she'd had to deal with her father. He was proud of her spunk, but really angry. "Where was your sense? You should have left the barn as soon as you thought someone was there." By then her mother had thought of all the grim things that could have happened. She'd made her own speech too.

After breakfast Jenny had phoned. Dr. Harris had told Joanna, "There was enough rat poison in the feed to kill the foal and likely the mare too." Since the stable was closed on Monday, Jenny had insisted that Lucy come over to the shop. She and Joanna wanted to hear the story minute by minute. Joanna had come over to the house for Lucy, because she also wanted a few words with Mrs. Hill.

At the Saddlery Monday afternoon Jenny and her

mother had both listened intently, with Jenny interrupting all the time to ask for details. She'd say, "What were you feeling right then?" or "Did you think of doing such and such?" Joanna had seemed more and more upset. Finally she'd said, "Much as I love Kaelie, what would I have done if something had happened to you?"

The rest of Monday Lucy had helped to inventory the merchandise for Rock Ridge. Every now and then Joanna would give her an unexpected hug. Around lunchtime Jenny had said, "I've acted out the whole scene in my head. I would never have thought of letting the horses out. You're smart, Lucy. As smart as your brother, whatever your mother thinks." So everything was fine between her and the Lovetts, but that wasn't the end.

Tuesday was Mr. Kendrick's turn. He would never go on and on like her parents, but his message was clear. It's one thing to trust yourself, and another to take on more than you can handle.

Later the police came over to the house. They never said straight out that she'd been foolish, but it wasn't hard to tell that's what they thought. They'd asked her to describe the man at the barn. She hadn't really seen him very clearly, so she wasn't much help.

Now it was Wednesday and she'd thought hard about what everyone had said. She sat up and looked at the clock on her night table. She'd better not miss her ride to the stable. But she still had to decide what *she* thought. Next time she'd try to think faster and get out of trouble's way. But she could honestly say she'd been about to leave the annex when the man came out of the feed room. Once she'd been trapped, it was hard to know what to do. She'd used her head, and she'd saved Kaelie. All in all, she felt good about herself.

• • •

Jenny was pacing the parking area when Lucy arrived. Lucy ran up to her right away. "What's happened?" she asked.

"You mean you can tell? Mom got another phone call this morning. I heard the tape she took to the police." Jenny started to imitate the gruff voice: " 'We know your store will have a booth at the Rock Ridge Horse Show. Make sure the picture is there. Put it where we can see it, but *do not sell* it.' " She tired of the act. "A messenger will show up sometime Saturday. He'll ask for 'the picture that's on loan.' Then we're supposed to hand it over."

"This is awful."

"It gets worse. He warned Mom again not to go to the police and he said the picture had better be there. Otherwise, something will happen 'that we'll never forget.' "

Lucy said, "Keep me company so we can keep on talking. I've got to get Triumph."

"No, you don't. Sally said we're riding together with Mr. Kendrick at two o'clock. It's a last brush-up for the show."

"Then let's go down to the ring and watch your regular class. I learn a lot."

As they started down the drive, Lucy asked, "What does Lee say about all this?"

Jenny made a face. "Mom told him about the first call and he was very concerned. He said that he and Dean would contact the original dealer to find out what was going on. But since the attack on Kaelie the other night, Mom won't speak to him. Whoever's after that picture, Lee must be feeding them information. How else would these creeps know about Kaelie and where to find her stall? How else would they know about the booth at Rock Ridge?"

Lucy clamped her teeth to keep herself from defending Lee. Jenny would just burn. "So what did the police say?"

"The chief of detectives asked a lot of questions. He really listened and said he'd get back to Mom with some kind of a plan. He's also trying to get in touch with Mr. Shields in Europe."

"Jenny, I'm so sorry that you and your mother are going through this." It was hard to see Jenny with a pale face and tired eyes.

"You know what makes it worse? Mom seems to think she'll get the picture back from Mr. Shields and just give it to Lee to return to the person who wants it. She thinks that will end the whole thing. She's been so upset, I don't think she cares about catching the person who's responsible for all this. She just wants to forget it."

"Whatever you think about Lee, your mother liked him a lot. She's got to be unhappy that it's ending this way."

"I suppose you're right. But I'm glad she told him not to phone anymore."

Lucy decided to say what she thought about Lee just once, whether Jenny got angry or not.

"I know, Jenny, that Lee looks really bad here," she said. "But I like him a lot. I think he's very kind. We've seen it. I can't believe he would mastermind break-ins and killing a horse or anything like that. Besides, he gave us the pictures in the first place."

Jenny stopped walking and faced Lucy. "Mom and I have been all through that. She doesn't think Lee is trying to get the picture for himself. She thinks he's helping the people who want it. Maybe they've put some kind of pressure on him. But she can't go on liking a man who's on the crooks' side instead of hers."

They started to walk again, but every so often Jenny kicked at the dirt with her boots. Finally she said, "To tell the truth, I think my mother is protecting Lee. He didn't start calling her until the day the blond man showed up in the shop. I don't know why he gave us the pictures, but I think he's in this all the way."

Lucy bit her tongue. Jenny was still winding down: "You know how I can pretend almost anything. Maybe Lee's a good actor too. We found out at Just Desserts that he used to act in Gilbert and Sullivan at school. I think—"

Lucy's mind wandered off. It was crazy. They were going on like Sherlock Holmes and Dr. Watson, but this case was real. If something awful happened, it would happen to real people.

"Jenny, your mother can't get hold of the picture by Saturday. Tell me again. What did they say they'd do if it wasn't there?"

"Exact words: 'Something will happen that you'll never forget.' But, I told you, the police are working out a plan. They'll have to tell us about it soon. The show's in two days."

"Well, I guess we can leave it to them."

"That's a good one, coming from you! Anyway, Lucy, please! Let's forget it for now."

They walked over to the Main Ring, where Liz was just cantering into the second row of fences. Jenny said, "I'm not as gung ho as you, but I'd still like to win a blue ribbon for Curtain Call on Saturday. Dad was so proud when he bought that horse for me."

"I'm sure you will, Jen. I hope Michael will do well too."

"He will! That kid just has the right genes."

"Mr. Kendrick's going to tell us today if he thinks Michael's ready."

"Michael's all excited because you're 'pretending a horse show' for his lesson." The bounce was back in her voice. "I'll come, too, and play the judge."

● ● ●

In the stable yard that afternoon Lucy put a saddle on Pirate and fastened the girth loosely. Steve Bolton passed by on his way to the office. "I hear you and Jenny are going to Rock Ridge. You were looking good out there a little while ago."

"Thanks." Why did her voice have to wobble just because a boy said something nice? As she watched Steve walk away, Michael rammed into her with a big hug. Jenny came along behind him.

As they all started down to the Beginners' Ring, Sally called from the office door. "Wait up. You've got a message."

Sally caught up with Jenny. "Your mother called. You're supposed to ask Lucy to arrange to come back to the Saddlery with you and Michael. Something to do with special instructions for Rock Ridge."

Jenny gave Lucy a pointed look. It must be a meeting with the detective.

"I'll meet you at the ring," Lucy said to Michael. "Let Jenny get you started."

It took Lucy a while to get off the phone. Her mother

thought she was spending too much time at the Lovetts', and Lucy wasn't about to mention a detective. She'd already seen one policeman this week. But they worked it out, and Lucy hurried down the drive.

Michael was already circling the ring at a walk. He had wonderful balance and his little legs were strong enough to stay in place. For a five-year-old his hands were surprisingly gentle. If he kept at it, he had the makings of a real rider.

Lucy opened the gate and strode into the center of the ring. "All right, Michael. We're going to pretend that we're at the show. When you enter the ring, you'll walk Pirate in the same direction as everyone else. There'll be a lot of other riders around you. What did we practice with Liz's class?"

"Don't bunch up."

"Right. So what did I tell you to do?"

"Go away. Cross all the way over sometimes."

"Right. Remember that. Now, after you walk awhile, the announcer will say, *'Prepare to trot.'* You shorten your reins and make sure Pirate is paying attention. Show me. Good. And now, *trot, please.*"

"Oops. Wrong diagonal," Lucy said, but Michael had already sat to one stride and changed it. Lucy let him trot for a while, correcting a few things here and there. Then she said suddenly, "Now you're right on top of that pony in front of you. Show me what you'll do. Remember, Jenny is the judge."

Michael pulled on his inside rein and headed Pirate across the ring. He stayed a safe distance from Jenny and, when he reached the other side, took the track in the right direction.

Lucy was delighted. They went on working hard for

almost half an hour—changing directions in the ring, trying not to cut corners, and working on diagonals. Occasionally Jenny had something to say, but she never interfered.

"Now we're going to try something new," Lucy said. "I'm going to stand outside the ring, the way I'll do at the show. I'll be there, Michael, all the time. But you're not supposed to look at me. Remember, look straight ahead or in the direction you're turning."

Mr. Kendrick walked up to Lucy at the rail. "Sorry I missed the beginning of his lesson," he said. Then he watched without speaking for about five minutes. "Lots of promise here," he said finally. "I can see that he's tired now. But he has control of the horse and he's secure in the saddle. I think we'll let him try it."

"See you at Rock Ridge, Michael," he called.

Michael was so excited, he turned his pony into the ring and trotted across to Lucy.

Jenny jumped out of the way quickly. "This time you did it," she called to her brother. "Never mind the judge, you almost ran over your sister."

Everyone laughed together, including Mr. Kendrick.

• • •

Lucy and Jenny were in the back of the Saddlery attaching price tags while they waited for the detective. Joanna was in her office. Michael sat on the floor in the children's corner, bent over a wooden puzzle of two horses in a field.

"Lucy, Lucy, I finished the black horse. Come look," Michael called.

"In a minute."

The minute stretched to ten minutes at least. Suddenly Lucy thought she heard the high-pitched bleats of the Touch-Tone phone. She hurried to the front of the store. Michael was holding the receiver in his hand.

"I should never have taught you that," Lucy said crossly. "Never, never use the phone in the Saddlery. Get Jen or me if you need to call someone. And what did you promise me, even at home?"

"I was careful," Michael said. "I played nine two two. I didn't call the firemen."

He was so adorable, it was hard to remain stern. Lucy used her firmest voice. "Michael, you're not listening. Never play your tunes without permission. It was our secret, remember? You promised."

He hung his head and went back to the puzzle. Then the sleigh bells rang. A man walked in wearing a tan Windbreaker and carrying a package under his arm.

"Hello, Miss Lovett," he said. "I'm Lieutenant Norton."

"I'm Lucy Hill, sir. That's Jenny over there."

Jen joined them quickly, and Joanna too. "Hello, Lieutenant," Joanna said. "You've been seeing quite a lot of us. I'll put the closing sign on the door."

"Not necessary, Mrs. Lovett. I won't stay long. Just long enough to make sure everyone understands."

The clever part of Lieutenant Norton's plan, Lucy thought, was borrowing Mr. Kendrick's print to hang in the booth. That's what he'd been carrying in the package. There'd be two plainclothes detectives watching the booth at all times during the three days of the show. They weren't to be spoken to unless they came up to the booth as customers, but Lucy, Jen, and Joanna would be introduced to them before Friday. The picture would be hung on the back "wall" of the booth, as instructed, and marked sold. If the "messenger" came for the picture, he would use the agreed-upon words: "Give me the picture that's on loan." When the picture was delivered, the detectives would take over.

Lucy wondered about the plan. The pictures were hard to tell apart unless they were next to each other. But there were differences if you knew where to look, like the number of horses in the jump line at the back fence. Would the messenger see through the trick? The detectives thought not. She hoped they were right.

Chapter Eleven

Setting up the booth at Rock Ridge on Saturday, the second day of the show, had gone much faster than on the first. At a quarter to eight Lucy and Jenny went to look for the horse van. Behind them the loudspeakers were testing one-two-three. Riders in the early equitation classes were warming up in the schooling area with their trainers. More vans and trailers were joining those from the day before in a large field at some distance from the rings.

"They should be here by now." Jenny looked up the road that led into the grounds. "Curtain Call is so hard to load. He hates getting in or out of the van. I wish I'd been there."

"We were sleepwalking this morning as it was!"

Friday, the first day of the show, had been long and tiring. They'd arrived at the show grounds at seven A.M. to set up the booth. By the first class everything had looked just right and Joanna had been pleased with the new friends she'd made for the shop and the amount of business they'd done.

Whenever they could, Lucy and Jenny had watched a

class or two. But most of the time they'd watched the detectives. At least one of the men had been in sight at all times. Since Gruff Voice had mentioned calling for the picture on Saturday, no one was especially tense. But it had been a good dress rehearsal.

By the time they'd reached Westlake last night, the three of them had been starving. They'd stopped at the Greek diner for a late supper. Then she and Jenny still had to braid manes and tails for Triumph, Curt, and Pirate. They'd used a bright blue wool on the pony, which looked spiffy with light gray. The two horses were in green, a terrific color for Triumph's deep brown coat.

Lucy had collapsed into bed at midnight, but her alarm was set for five A.M. This morning she'd pulled on her jeans with her eyes closed. Her show clothes were on hangers in the rented van.

"They'll be here," Lucy said to Jenny, who had started pacing up and down. "None of us has a class before lunch."

"I just have a funny feeling about today."

"Of course. It isn't at every horse show where you're cooperating with detectives and waiting for a crook between classes."

"Let's go back to Mom. She was okay with Michael asleep in a chair. When he wakes up she'll need at least one of us just for him. He's so excited, I hope he remembers a walk from a trot."

The green-and-white tents for the refreshments and the specialty vendors, such as the Fairfax Saddlery, were on the opposite side of the show rings. As they walked up to their booth, Lucy thought again that it looked fabulous. A brightly colored banner with the name and insignia of the Saddlery was stretched across the front. The merchandise was arranged in bright metal shelves along the side "walls." Joanna had bought a screen to put across the back on which she'd put hangers with a few jackets, breeches, and shirts. Mr. Kendrick's hunt scene hung in the center.

Lucy spotted Rudy, the detective with the receding hairline. He was dressed like one of the trainers or a father working with the horses. He was consulting a prize list.

As Joanna arranged a few small items at the front of the table, Lucy studied the picture above her head. Most customers gave it a look. That added to the tension. The messenger would probably look like just anybody. The detectives certainly did.

"Mom, you'd better stay at the booth with us every minute," Jen said. "I'll be so busy trying to decide if a customer's the messenger, I won't be able to write up a sales slip."

"I'll be right here," Joanna said reassuringly, but she didn't look so calm herself.

"There's not much business yet. Let's see if the van's here now," Jen said. "I'd rather worry about that."

Lucy and Jenny strode across the show grounds, enjoying their surroundings too much for conversation. Early morning at a show was a special pleasure, when the gray light was just lifting and expectation made sights and sounds more vivid.

Close to the van and trailer area Jen started to run. "There's Freddie, coming this way. Maybe he's looking for us."

"Hi, Freddie!" Lucy waved.

Freddie didn't look happy to see them. "Is something the matter?" Jenny asked.

"Jennifer, I'm sorry. We know to watch out for that horse, but a loud horn surprised him coming down the ramp and he slipped."

Jen turned white. "How bad is it?"

"Hey, he'll be fine. He took a chunk out of his pastern on the right leg just above the hoof. I was on my way for the show vet. The thing is, I don't think you'll be able to ride him today."

• • •

An hour later Jenny was beginning to be grateful that Curt wasn't seriously hurt, even if she was disappointed about losing her chance to show. Of course her hunter classes were out, but Lucy tried to persuade her to ride Triumph for equitation, where the rider was judged and not the horse.

"Go for the mileage, Jen. It's all good practice."

"But I've been up on that horse just once for exactly ten minutes."

"So? Mr. Kendrick will be here, and so am I. We'll work in the schooling area. Besides, you've watched me ride him often enough."

Jenny gave her a warm smile. "You've got classes too. And the horse has to look good for those buyers Mr. Kendrick wants to attract. He'll never say yes."

But Mr. Kendrick did say yes, for two classes—Open on the flat and Open over fences.

By ten-thirty the show grounds were quite crowded. There were classes in the large and small rings, and sometimes hunter classes on the outside course too. The grandstand was filling up at one side of the big ring and the reserved spaces for cars the rest of the way around.

Lucy and Jenny took turns dealing with Michael, taking him off to watch a jumping class or to see the big vans in the stabling area. Without fail, whoever came back to the booth asked the same question: "Do you think the messenger was here?"

Joanna's answer was always no. But around eleven-thirty her face was ashen. "Stay with me, one of you, please."

"What's wrong, Mom?"

"I—I think the messenger was here. I think it was a woman and I think she knew this wasn't the right print."

"Are you sure?"

"Sure enough."

"What's going to happen if you're right?"

"The detectives are here, and what terrible thing could take place in public at a horse show?"

"That's what my father said when he agreed to let me come." Lucy bit her tongue. Joanna had insisted she tell her parents the whole story, but Lucy didn't want her to think there'd been any hassle.

"Don't worry, girls. I was just a little shaken." Joanna looked over at Michael. His straight blond hair fell over his face as he patted a customer's Jack Russell terrier. "Let's make sure Michael is close to one of us at all times. Don't let him talk to strangers. And be extra careful when he's on the pony."

At noon Jenny took Michael off to the minivan to help him get dressed. She changed into her show clothes, too, and they made quite a picture when they came back to the booth in their matching jackets and hunt caps. When Lucy had changed, the three of them went to the horse van for Pirate. Freddie tightened the girth and put Michael in the saddle. Then they led him to the schooling area to warm up.

Mr. Kendrick came along a little later, but let Lucy continue to work with Michael herself. Lucy was beginning to get excited. She could tell from the number of young children that the class was going to be big. "No bunching up, Michael. Remember!" He didn't seem nervous at all.

When the class was called to the small ring, Michael and Pirate were already at the ingate. Lucy let one or two riders enter the ring first, then sent Michael in behind them. Unfortunately Joanna was stuck at the booth, but Lucy joined Jenny at the rail. Michael looked wonderful, with his straight back, his balanced seat, and his serious face.

The class went well at the walk. Michael remembered not to cut corners and moved his pony along. In the distance Lucy heard the purr of a helicopter. It seemed to be heading for the show grounds. Maybe it was going to come down in one of the large fields beyond the stabling area. Lucy had heard of parents arriving that way.

"Prepare to trot," the ring steward said. Good. Michael had shortened his reins. *"And trot, please."* Great! On the right diagonal and in front of the judge. She smiled across the ring to Mr. Kendrick, even though he couldn't see her.

At her shoulder Jen said, "That copter is definitely coming here. The noise is going to panic the horses if it doesn't stay up high."

Lucy looked up for a second. Around her, other people were looking up too. But she quickly turned her eyes back to Michael in the ring.

"Lucy," Jen said, "there are usually numbers on a copter, but I don't see them. Hey! What's he doing!"

The helicopter swooped down over the main ring. There was one horse on course but many more waiting their turn near the ingate. The blades twirled on over the smaller ring filled with children. The noise was outrageous. So was the wind and dust. Some of the horses turned their heads straight up. Others reared and followed their instinct to run from danger. In seconds the ring area was in turmoil. Lucy and Jen ducked under the fence as Pirate whirled in a circle, and bolted. Michael fell off and sat on the ground looking up at the copter. Mr. Kendrick reached him first and lifted him over the rail to be sure he wouldn't be kicked or trampled. Joanna, by now only steps away, grabbed him.

Lucy ran to catch the pony as Jenny and Mr. Kendrick joined the other trainers trying to quiet the animals and to make sure the children were safe. When she looked up again, the copter was hovering. A booming voice announced from above: "Attention, ladies and gentleman. Thought you'd like to know. You can thank the Fairfax Saddlery for this one." Then the copter took off as fast as it could go.

A few minutes later the Show Manager spoke through the loudspeakers: "Our apologies to all of you for this terrible occurrence. We trust no one is hurt, but the first-aid station and the veterinarian's office are behind the grandstand. Let me hasten to say that every vendor at this show has been thoroughly investigated by the Horse Show Committee. The owner of the Fairfax Saddlery has been known to us since she was a Junior Rider. She is a person of outstanding character who would have nothing to do with this ugly demonstration. A police investigation is already under way. Now let's get back to our business. Ten minutes of music will permit everyone to bring matters under control. Then Green Jumpers will continue in the Main Ring. In the Second Ring, Walk Trot under Eight."

While Jenny held the pony, Lucy hurried to Joanna and Michael. Remember what happened to Grace Zampkin, she thought. Don't give him a choice. Here's your chance to get it right.

"Michael," she said, dropping to his level. "The class is going to begin again and Pirate is waiting. He was very frightened by something he didn't understand. As frightened as you. You have to get back up there and help him get his courage back."

She stood up and held out her hand, looking at Joanna in case she disapproved. Michael ran toward Pirate so fast, she could hardly keep up. She was thinking that she'd certainly done it right this time when he turned and called to her. "Look. Lucy, Pirate isn't scared. He's like me. I wasn't much scared. Lucy, come on!"

When the class was over, Michael left the ring with a bright red ribbon.

• • •

For Lucy the rest of the afternoon felt like one of her father's thirty-second commercials with everything in clipped scenes. Joanna went back to the booth, joined by a good friend who happened to be at the show. Lieutenant Norton showed up and the detectives stayed. Some people came by just to see what Joanna looked like and others to express concern. Business was fair. Since Joanna was no longer alone, Lucy and Jenny tried to concentrate on schooling and riding their classes.

Considering that this had been a rotten day from the start, everything went quite well. Freddie had been near the ring with Triumph during the helicopter raid, because Lucy's first class, Novice on the flat, was right after Michael's. *Novice* meant only contestants who'd won fewer than three blues. It was hard to get the horse's attention so soon after the excitement, but Lucy won a second like Michael.

When they drew lots for jumping order in Novice over fences, Lucy discovered there were more than thirty contestants. With that kind of competition she had little chance of a ribbon. She relaxed about winning and focused on making Triumph look good. There might be a buyer out there!

When she left the ring, Jenny ran up with a broad grin. "You went clean. That was great!" Only then did Lucy believe it. She patted the big horse. "Good for you, Triumph, you're an ace when it counts." She started to dismount, but Freddie stopped her. "Mr. Kendrick said to stick around." In a class this big they usually brought a small group of riders back for another look.

Lucy could feel her heart beating against her chest. Jenny and Freddie waited with her, but no one said a word. All eyes were on the ring, appraising each rider in turn and calculating Lucy's chances.

At last the judges tallied their score cards and walked out to the show stand. Minutes later the loudspeaker blared, "The following riders will jump again in this order." The ring attendants began to raise three of the fences as the numbers were read: 50, 2, 12, 79 . . . 79! That's me, Lucy realized. That's me!

Mr. Kendrick hurried over a few minutes before Lucy's turn in the ring. "There was a nice rhythm to that round, the best you've done with that horse. Just do the same things again."

There was no way to feel as relaxed this time, but Lucy tried. Toward the end of the ride she realized that she was concentrating on how many jumps were left instead of setting up Triumph to get over them. His hooves ticked a rail on the next to last fence, but it didn't move.

Again there was the wait while five more riders took their turns. Then the judges marked their cards and the announcer came to the mike: "And we have the winners of Class Fifteen, Novice over fences: First, number fifty, Susan Philips; second, number twelve, Edward Stern; third, Lucy Hill, number seventy-nine . . ."

Lucy heard the rest as a blur. A few minutes later she trotted into the ring to collect a yellow ribbon for third place. Much as she'd hoped to come home with a blue, this was much tougher competition than she'd ridden against before. And later she won a sixth in Limit on the flat. That class included riders who'd won up to *six* blues in different shows. All in all the future looked bright.

Triumph did well for Jenny too. Only beginning to get the feel of him in her first class, she still won a third. During her last class, Open over fences, Joanna came to the ring to watch. Lucy stood beside her.

As Jenny moved from fence to fence, Lucy knew just how far she had to go ever to be as good as her friend. When Jen came out of the ring, she walked Triumph to keep him loose, while Lucy and Joanna watched the competition at the rail.

All of a sudden Lee Cotter appeared at Joanna's elbow. Numbed by the day, Joanna looked up at him without any reaction at all.

"I heard a bulletin on the local radio," Lee said.

"This is dreadful, Joanna. I'm so sorry." He put an arm around her shoulders, but she backed away.

Lucy started to move farther down the rail. "Lucy, I wish you would stay," Joanna said quickly. Lucy stood where she was, trying not to look at either of them.

Joanna turned away from the ring. "Lee, I've made it clear that I want nothing to do with you. After today, whatever vestige of feeling I have left . . ." She stopped there. A few beats later she said, "If you care at all, just give me the name of the dealer who sold you and Dean the prints. Then I can give it to the police. But obviously someone made sure those people had all the information they needed to wreck this day and possibly the future of the Saddlery too."

Lee looked as if he'd been slapped. His cheek began to twitch. After a very long pause he said, "The pictures came from D. Builder and Sons in Chatham, New York." He turned to Lucy. "I'm glad to see you, Lucy." Then he walked away.

Jenny won the class. That was about all that Lucy registered for the rest of the day except later, back home, when she put the new ribbons on her lampshade.

Chapter Twelve

"**W**ere there any customers at the Saddlery at all yesterday?" Mr. Hill asked Lucy as she came into the kitchen for breakfast Tuesday morning. He folded his *New York Times*.

"A few, but Monday's never particularly busy." Lucy filled a bowl with dry cereal and took the milk from the refrigerator. "Dad, do you think people are really going to hold the helicopter raid against Joanna? So many people know her in the town. Won't they give her the benefit of the doubt?"

"Some people will, of course. But this incident was so extreme. Most people will remember the helicopter, connect the unpleasantness with Joanna, and stop there. Of course, if there is something valuable hidden in that frame at her lawyer's and if the police trace the criminals, the story will run in the *Westlaker*. That should help some."

Lucy joined her father at the table with her cereal, but left the spoon in its place. "The police are in touch with Mr. Shields's office. They expect to hear from him today. The chief of detectives was at the Saddlery yesterday for the longest time. He asked Joanna more about where the pictures came from and—"

"Now they have a real crime to work on."

"Because of the helicopter, you mean. It's not just my idea about the picture anymore, or some voice on the phone."

"Exactly. And now they know that you're probably right. There must be a large amount of money involved here somehow. People don't run around buzzing horse shows in helicopters for small stakes."

Mr. Hill put down his napkin and picked up the newspaper. "I'm taking you to the stable this morning. Meet you seven minutes from now at the front door." He kissed the top of her head and left the room.

Lucy toyed with the cereal. Even though Rock Ridge was seventy-five miles away, lots of people seemed to be talking about the helicopter. This could mean the end of the Saddlery. And what might these vicious people do next? Joanna hadn't smiled even once in the last two days.

• • •

When Lucy walked into the stable office, Mr. Kendrick was signing some letters at Sally's desk. "Good morning, Lucy," he said. "I'd like a few minutes with you when I finish here."

"Sure, Mr. Kendrick."

Lucy waited beside Widget at the corner of the desk. She scratched the cat behind an ear. What could this be about? Mr. Kendrick had already given her some fine compliments about Saturday.

Mr. Kendrick put down the pen and said, "Well, Lucy, I had a phone call this morning from a Mr.

Pandolfino, who was at Rock Ridge with his children on Saturday. The little girl was in Michael's Walk Trot class, and there's also a boy of twelve. He's going to buy Triumph for his son."

Mr. Kendrick was obviously pleased and Lucy tried to smile. She squinted her eyes to hold back tears. It was going to be hard to part with the only horse she'd had a chance to pretend was hers.

"Uh—well, I knew from the beginning that he was here to be sold." She wished she could get the quaver out of her voice. She'd wanted to do a good job and she had. Though it was probably Jenny's blue-ribbon class that had clinched it.

"You accomplished just what I asked. Mr. Pandolfino will bring his son over in a few days to ride the horse himself, but I'm sure the deal is done. He was most impressed by your first classes after the helicopter. He thought the horse had settled down remarkably well and had a nice way of going."

"And then he saw Jenny's class too."

"No, he left at about two o'clock. The little girl was upset by the helicopter and he wanted to get her home." Mr. Kendrick smiled in his special way, with the deep lines around his mouth. It was as though he'd read her mind.

"Let's step outside a minute," he went on. "There's something else I want to talk to you about."

Mr. Kendrick held the screen door open for her and they went out into the sunlight. As they walked a little way, Mr. Kendrick continued, "You've worked hard at your riding this summer. You'll miss Triumph, I know, but he's taught you about all he can. And I'll be able to find other horses for you to work with, certainly by next summer. You've got a lot of talent. What I'd like to avoid is that winter break we've had each year."

"So-o would I," Lucy said vigorously. "But my mother—my parents are afraid it will interfere with my schoolwork. And, well, the money's a part of it too."

"The schoolwork is up to you. But I can work out something for you here, with chores or assistant teaching to help take care of your lessons."

There was no way to hide her excitement. Mr. Kendrick looked at her kindly. "Think it over, Lucinda, and talk to your folks." He gave her a pat on the shoulder and walked back toward the office.

For a time Lucy stood just where she was, replaying the conversation in her head over and over again. Then she hurried to Triumph's stall.

"So you're going to leave me," she said, feeling his soft nose under her hand. "You gave me a hard time for a while, but we got to be friends." This time she felt her tears on her cheek. "Thanks, fella, for teaching me so much. I'll never forget you. And now Mr. Kendrick's really going to help me. When I win the Maclay, I'll find you and tell you about it. You'll see."

Suddenly Lucy remembered talking to Triumph the day they'd found Widget in the file drawer. She'd been so full of her own feelings just now, she'd forgotten all about Jenny's troubles.

She gave Triumph's ear a pull. "I swore I'd get to the bottom of that mystery, remember? Well, I didn't. The bottom's much deeper than I thought. No one knows what will happen next. I just wish the police would move faster. Jenny hates to see her mother this unhappy. The other day she even said, 'I guess I can't expect my mother to live alone all the rest of her life.' "

Lucy could feel the frustration building up inside of her. She hated these people who'd sold the pictures to Lee and Dean.

Lee and Dean. Lee and Dean. Everyone always talked about them together. Everyone put the blame on them together. Maybe that was a mistake. She wondered if Dean was at all like Lee and tried to remember what she knew about him. His passion was clocks. Maybe he knew how to fix them. Maybe he was good at locks and burglar alarms too.

With a surge of elation Lucy clapped Triumph on the neck. "I've got to go to Carousel Antiques. I've got to get a lift up there. I'll be very careful. I'll just feel things out with Lee. But who will take me?"

The horse tossed his head and blew through his nose.

"Too bad I don't understand your language."

Liz passed by, carrying a saddle and bridle from the tack room. Maybe the horse was talking to her after all.

"Say, Liz, do you have any reason to drive up to Geddings?"

"Sure, Lucy, from time to time."

"Uh—I don't suppose this is one of the times."

"Not really. Why?"

"I need a lift very badly. I'll do some barn chores for you, Liz. I'll clean stalls, fill water buckets, sweep aisles, anything you say, if you'll just run me up there and bring me back—even just half an hour later."

Liz looked at her curiously. "I wouldn't be getting you into any trouble, would I? No boyfriend, or anything like that?"

Lucy could feel herself turning red. "No. No. It's an

antiques store I'm going to. It's—it's a surprise for my father."

"I'll tell you what. If you can go at eleven o'clock and stay only half an hour so I'm back for my two o'clock, I'll do it. I'm going to need some time off in the next few weeks. I'll be glad for your help."

"Anything!" Lucy said.

• • •

Lucy had always felt that Liz was a special person and the drive together, for more than an hour, meant a chance to know more about her. They talked about how hard it was to become a very good competitive rider without lots of money. But Liz gave her hope. She'd done well by trading work and teaching for lessons.

Liz said, "When you're good enough and people can count on you, Lucy, they'll let you ride their horses and even show them."

She stopped at an intersection. "We're almost there. Do you know how to get to this antiques shop once we get to Geddings?"

"Straight through the village and a few blocks farther. It's in a big white house with a merry-go-round horse in front."

"Good. I'll drop you there and do my errands. Half an hour, okay?"

Driving along, she'd been thinking about what she'd say to Lee. Had she gone too far in coming up here? What about all those scoldings and the promises she'd made to herself?

But Lee had been happy to talk to her at Rock Ridge. He'd probably be glad to see her, if only to find out about Joanna. She could always say something again about a present for her dad. She wasn't actually putting herself in danger this time, maybe just being too nosy. But if she could help solve the problem for the Lovetts, it was worth it.

Liz stopped in front of the house and Lucy jumped out before she could get cold feet. It was only about three weeks ago that she'd been here with Joanna and Jenny. All the trouble had started so simply. Walking up the path, she remembered that she'd been the one to spy the first picture. How she wished she hadn't.

The door to the house opened and Lee said a few words to a man who was leaving. The man walked down the path toward her. He was so deep in thought that he noticed nothing around him, but Lucy's stomach turned over.

In the doorway Lee said, "Why, hello, Lucy, come in, come in."

The man walking down the path toward her was the tall blond man who'd come to the Fairfax Saddlery.

Chapter Thirteen

As Lucy stepped into the house, her whole body felt cold. What had she gotten herself into now? If Lee and the tall blond man were friends, she'd made a dreadful mistake. And now she might be alone with Lee for at least half an hour.

"Lucy! You're as white as that ironstone platter. Whatever's the matter?" His dark eyes were kind, but he seemed keyed up about something.

"Uh—I'm fine, Lee. When I was here last time I saw a present my father might like for his birthday. If I can afford it, I mean." Lucy tried to remember even one object. "Uh, it was an old brass inkwell. You had a quill pen sitting in it."

Lee was looking at her strangely. Lucy tried to edge toward the door.

"Well, let's look around for that inkwell. Perhaps we can work something out."

Lucy stood where she was. "Lee, the man you were talking to before. He looks—sort of familiar. Could I have seen him somewhere? Around the stable sometime? Or—or—does he own a restaurant I might have gone to with my folks. I think I've—"

"That's my brother Dean, Lucy."

"Your brother! But you don't look at all alike." No wonder she'd never thought the blond man could be Dean.

"We're half brothers, you see."

"I remember now. Joanna told us."

"Lucy, there's something on your mind besides an old inkwell. Why are you asking about Dean? Does he have something to do with the way you looked when you came in?"

Lee's voice reminded her of the day at Just Desserts when he'd been so patient with Michael. She decided to take a chance.

"You remember when Joanna came up here with Jenny and me, the day we bought the three pictures?"

"Of course I do. I'm most unhappy that those prints have created so many problems for Joanna."

"We didn't meet Dean that day, because he was away at some kind of a sale."

"Yes, in Houston."

"Well, a few days later he came down to the Saddlery. He asked for Joanna and when she wasn't there, he said he was looking for a present for his niece. But I didn't think he was. There was something strange about it. Jenny told him—"

"Just a minute, Lucy. Dean hasn't got a niece. This is very serious. I knew nothing about this—"

"But you know that someone broke into the Saddlery that same night?"

"Wasn't it a false alarm?"

"That's what people thought for a while. But you see,

Jenny told the blond man—I mean Dean—that we'd had three terrific prints and they'd walked right out of the shop. We think—uh—that Dea—someone broke into the shop that night to get into the sales slips and find out where the pictures had gone. Dean had been looking at the jewelry by the front counter for a very long time. He could have been watching to see where we put the slips when we finished with the customers."

Lee looked terrible. Not white like the platter, but gray. "Lucy, we don't need to stand by the door. Please come in and sit down." She hesitated, but Lee looked as though he needed a chair badly. She followed him to a room off the hall.

Lee gripped the arms of his chair. It was almost as though he were talking to himself as he went on. "When Dean came back from Houston, he found out, of course, that I'd sold the two prints from the workshop to Joanna. I could see that he was very upset. I thought it was because I took the pictures from the workshop when he was still working on them. He started to lose his temper but controlled himself immediately. Now I realize that he didn't want to seem *too* worked up about two inexpensive prints. I'd have begun to ask questions. He must have realized that the first thing to do was to try and buy them back from Joanna."

Lee leaned back in his chair and went off into thought. Finally he said, "Dean also canceled his trip to London. Now I know the reason. He had to get the pictures back first. What makes you think Dean looked at the invoices? Did someone try to steal the other two pictures?"

"Not to steal them, but to look at them. The burglar knew which picture he wanted. The one in Mr. Kendrick's apartment wasn't the right one. Neither was the one at Perfect Pictures."

Lee rubbed the back of his hand across his forehead. "The first I heard of any of this was after Joanna received that threatening phone call. When she told me about it, I went to Dean immediately. I asked him to speak to the people who'd sold him the prints to find out what was going on and if we should go to the police. That was about ten days ago. All I've been getting is double-talk. Dean and I were quarreling about that very thing when you arrived. And of course Joanna stopped speaking to me soon after, so I had no idea what was happening until the helicopter . . ." It was as though he couldn't go on.

"I was there, Lee, when you were talking to Joanna at Rock Ridge, remember? The same man with the gruff voice told her to have the picture there that day, or else. But she couldn't get the third picture because—"

Lee stood up abruptly. He reached over for Lucy's arm and pulled her out of her chair. "We've got to get out of here, Lucy. We've got to get to Joanna's right away."

"But my friend's coming back for me in about fifteen minutes."

"We'll put a note on the door." He reached into a nearby desk and handed Lucy paper and pen. "Write quickly. We've got to go. We still don't have the whole story, but that helicopter business was extreme. If Dean's part of all this, he's desperate to get his hands on that picture, and he doesn't have it yet. You can tell me more in the car. If he loses his temper, Joanna is in serious danger."

"You mean right now?"

"Right now. Joanna won't talk to me or I'd phone

and warn her. And I can't call the police. We're not even sure what he's up to. I've got to go down there myself."

"I—I still don't understand exactly."

"Dean made an appointment with Joanna to advise her about selling some of her paintings. She thought he'd be able to help her in London. He was on his way to Joanna's when he left here."

•••

Lee drove his car as fast as he dared and spoke very little on the way back to Westlake. Meanwhile Lucy filled him in on the parts of the story he didn't know. She felt bad about Liz, but she'd explain it all later the best she could.

After a while Lee said, "So, then, Joanna thought I was involved with the break-ins and the threats?"

"No. She blamed those things on the people who sold you the pictures. But she did think you were helping them with information."

"Oh?" She could see that he was upset.

"Well, someone knew all about Kaelie and where to find her stall. Someone knew we were going to Rock Ridge and that Joanna would have a booth there. Things like that."

Lee was gripping the steering wheel hard. His cheek began to twitch.

"How could I have been so blind? But Joanna had been as much Dean's friend as mine until a few weeks ago. When he asked me questions, I thought he was just showing interest."

A long silence followed. Finally he said, "Why would Joanna agree to see Dean after all that's happened? Why would she let Dean come to the house when she won't even talk to me?"

At first Lucy didn't answer. It wasn't her place to discuss anything like that. But it wasn't like Lee to be so open with someone her age either. She could see that it was only because he cared so much.

She thought awhile about how to put it. Then she said, "I think Joanna misses you. Maybe she hoped to find out something that would leave you in the clear."

Another long silence followed but after that, when they talked, they talked about other things.

● ● ●

Lee parked the car a few houses away from the Lovetts'. He suggested Lucy wait in the car, but the look on her face must have changed his mind. Together they walked along the edge of the property and quietly entered the house through the glass-enclosed porch off the living room. With Lee leading the way they moved close enough to see Dean standing near the fireplace and speaking wildly. They could hear him too.

"Thanks to my brother," he said, "my life isn't worth a snap of the fingers. You've had a sample of the way these guys do things. They know I owe them half a million dollars and they're tired of waiting. To make it right, Joanna, all you have to do is get the picture back, even for just a few days. What difference does it make to you anyway? You'll have the money I've offered you from my share. And I'll be off the hook."

Lee strode into the room. "Dean, what's this all about? How did you get into this kind of trouble? What's framed into that picture?"

Lucy edged her way into the room and stood toward

the back. Jenny, sitting next to her mother on the couch, gave her a desperate look. Dean was shouting, "If you'd kept out of it, Lee, I wouldn't be in this trouble. Keep out of it now."

"It's a Rembrandt drawing," Joanna answered. "A stolen drawing that Lee was going to take to his contact in London. Evidently—"

"Evidently you understand the situation well, Joanna. So why don't you just cooperate and fix it for all of us?"

Lee looked as though he was about to go for his brother's throat. "Lee, he's got a gun," Joanna said quietly.

Lucy looked at Jenny. Jen raised her eyebrows and nodded slightly. The next second Dean took his right hand out of his pocket. Lucy caught her breath when she saw the gun.

Suddenly she heard a sound behind her at the door to the library. Michael was peering into the room.

Dean saw her glance. "Don't think you're going out that way, young lady. Come right in here." He motioned toward the second couch with the gun.

Michael, his eyes fixed on the gun, stood in the doorway.

"Don't come in here, Michael," Lucy said in a low voice. "Go and play."

Lee saw Michael too. Trying to distract Dean, he said, "Did you try to poison Joanna's horse? Did you arrange that ugly scene at Rock Ridge?"

"Go and play, Michael," Lucy said again. Then suddenly she knew exactly what to say. "Go play your tunes. You don't have to be careful. You can play them *all.*"

Michael stood at the door, still looking at the gun.

But he seemed to be thinking. "I mean it," Lucy said. He gave her a look and scampered off.

Lucy hurried to the couch as ordered. Dean shouted at Lee, "You don't understand. My partners expect their cash fast. I stalled them at first while I looked for the print. But they're out half a million bucks. They got tired of waiting."

"Who got tired of waiting? Who are you tied up with here?"

"A syndicate that steals one or two pieces of art a year —master drawings and etchings."

Lee was edging closer to Dean, obviously intending to go for the gun. Joanna and Jenny were watching intently. But there wasn't anything they could do.

"I can't believe this, Dean," Lee said. "How long has it been going on? And what have you been doing with the money? Why haven't I seen any signs of it?"

"I don't have to play *Truth or Consequences* with you, Lee. Just get Joanna to listen to reason. It's as simple as that."

"I'll reason with her, Dean, but not while there's a gun to her head."

Lee started for the gun, but Dean kicked him away and pointed it firmly. "I came down here with a reasonable proposition. Joanna could ask for the picture back. Or she could tell me where to find it and my people would collect it. I don't like guns and you know it. But I'll use this if I have to."

Lee said, "Dean, I'll help you. I'll go with you to the police. Cooperate and we'll see what can be worked out. You—"

There was a loud knock at the door.

Dean jerked around. "Who's that?"

Lee lunged and grabbed his gun. "You don't want to hurt anyone, Dean."

Lucy caught her breath. Good boy, Michael! He'd "played" 911. This must be the police.

Chapter Fourteen

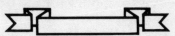

By Thanksgiving weekend Lucy's life was so changed that it was hard to remember the feeling of the summer days when she'd had hours to spend at the stable and with Jenny. This year at school she and Jen were even in different homeroom sections and almost never saw each other except at Up and Down Farm. But those intense weeks that had started at Carousel Antiques and ended with Michael's phone call to the police had made them closer friends than ever. They'd decided to meet at the Saddlery this afternoon. It was Sunday and they could do their homework together at the counter while Joanna took care of paperwork in the office.

Jenny finished first and went out for frozen yogurt. The sleigh bells jangled when she came back. "Well!" she said in Mrs. Wallace's voice. "No wonder my saddle hasn't come from France. The shop's turned into a schoolroom and a restaurant."

Lucy laughed and closed her science book. She took the yogurt from Jenny and as she began to eat, she looked around. The Saddlery was full of new and interesting things.

"Jen, am I seeing right? That picture in the back! I never thought you'd have another hunt scene here."

Jenny smiled. "I know what you mean. But when you think about it, the Carousel Antiques caper turned out pretty well in the end. For one thing, Mom certainly appreciated the reward money for the Rembrandt drawing."

Jenny would never have mentioned it, but Lucy had been rewarded too. The wonderful glass horse she used to admire was now on a shelf in her room, and she'd been promised a whole new set of show clothes next summer.

"Guess what," Jenny said. "Mom, Michael, and I are all going to visit Lee in San Francisco at Christmas."

"Hey! Luck-ee." Lucy dipped into the yogurt and tried not to be upset. "The way things are going, you'll probably move out there . . . someday."

Jenny shrugged her shoulders. "It wouldn't be so bad."

Lee had gone into partnership with a leading antiques shop in California and shipped the best of his inventory out there in October. Once he learned the truth about Dean's "fencing" for the art syndicate, he had no intention of continuing Carousel Antiques.

"I guess Lee will have to come back East for the trial," Lucy said.

"I'm sure, though he really never knew what was going on. Those people stole just a few things a year and Dean arranged to sell them in London. Since he was going there on business anyway, Lee had no idea. Lee says artwork stolen here is easier to unload overseas."

"Did he ever find out what Dean did with the money?"

"You won't believe it. He bought clocks. Small, precious clocks that he kept locked up at home and admired by himself."

"That's weird! So was he buying clocks that time in Houston?"

"No. That was an excuse. He was picking up another stolen etching. He planned to hide it behind the second picture Lee took from the workshop. Then he was going to take the two pictures to London a few days later."

Lucy scraped the bottom of the yogurt container slowly. Finally she said, "Jenny, maybe I shouldn't say this, but aren't you surprised sometimes at the way you and Lee get along now?"

Jenny thought a minute. "We do okay. I'm glad Mom and Michael are so happy, and I really do like him." She was quiet again. Lucy waited.

"For a long time I couldn't think about my father because I missed him so much. But now it makes me feel good to remember him. He was a great dad. And he's part of me. But I guess, if Mom married someone I really felt good about . . . well . . ."

She went back to her yogurt and said quickly, "Any new ideas for naming Kaelie's foal?"

"You know, Jenny, I've been meaning to ask you for ages. Where did Kaelie get that name? Does it mean something special?"

"It's Mom's version of the Irish word for a dance or get-together."

"That's special! Maybe we should wait to see if Kaelie drops a colt or a filly."

"Guess so. But if it's a boy, I vote for Napoleon."

Lucy looked puzzled.

"After the 'Six Napoleons,' the Sherlock Holmes story that helped us out."

As they both laughed, Lucy looked at her watch. "I'd better get ready. Mom will be here soon."

Jenny threw her hair over her face and went into an act. "Farewell, dear friend. I grieve your departure and await the morrow."

"The morrow after the morrow. The barn is closed on Mondays."

• • •

As Lucy stood outside in the nippy air, she thought: there's only one Jenny. It had been great to remember the summer. But this fall had been pretty special too. At school she was having the best time ever. Last year, she hadn't talked much in class, and whenever there was an oral report she'd got all flustered. Now she was beginning to wonder why it had seemed so hard. Even her written papers were better.

Eric thought it was because she had started to believe she had something to say. He was probably right. She had much more confidence since the summer. Both solving the mystery and everything she learned at the stable had helped with that. She thought a lot about that big lesson with Triumph when she'd been so scared. Now when she felt overwhelmed, she tried to turn the feeling into a challenge.

Her mother had agreed to the riding schedule as long as she kept up her grades. So she was working harder than ever at school. And she was working hard at the stable. The combination of chores and lessons meant giving up most extracurricular activities and also getting up very early in the morning to finish her homework. But nothing else was as important as the riding goals she'd set for herself. And just last week she'd been asked to exercise a valuable private horse for the first time.

In good weather, like today, Lee's parting present to Jenny stood in front of the Saddlery—the prancing merry-go-round horse with the wild eyes and rippling blue mane. Almost everyone who came or went gave it a pat and children climbed onto its back. Business had really picked up after Dean was arrested and the story came out. At this rate the horse would soon need new paint.

What would happen if Joanna married Lee and Jenny moved to San Francisco? It was hard to think about. Of course, she and Jenny could write letters and talk on the phone. They might even visit. But it wouldn't be the same.

She was getting to know Debby, the new girl at the stable. Debby could never be Jen, but "people were as different as horses," and when they knew each other better, they might end up good friends.

Mrs. Hill waved as she pulled up in front of the shop. Lucy gave the merry-go-round horse a good-night pat on the head. It was a good feeling to know she'd helped to put it there.

CELEBRATING
YEARLING
25 YEARS

Yearling Books
celebrates its
25 years—
and salutes
Reading Is
Fundamental®
on its 25th
anniversary.

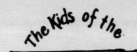

The Kids of the Polk Street School

Laugh with this funny class of sometimes *really* good, sometimes *really* mischievous boys and girls!

by Patricia Reilly Giff

- ☐ #1 **THE BEAST IN MS. ROONEY'S ROOM** 40485-1 $2.50
- ☐ #2 **FISH FACE** 42557-3 $2.75
- ☐ #3 **THE CANDY CORN CONTEST** 41072-X $2.75
- ☐ #4 **DECEMBER SECRETS** 41795-3 $2.50
- ☐ #5 **IN THE DINOSAUR'S PAW** 44150-1 $2.50
- ☐ #6 **THE VALENTINE STAR** 49204-1 $2.50
- ☐ #7 **LAZY LIONS, LUCKY LAMBS** 44640-6 $2.75
- ☐ #8 **SNAGGLE DOODLES** 48068-X $2.95
- ☐ #9 **PURPLE CLIMBING DAYS** 47309-8 $2.75
- ☐ #10 **SAY "CHEESE"** 47639-9 $2.75
- ☐ #11 **SUNNY SIDE UP** 48406-5 $2.75
- ☐ #12 **PICKLE PUSS** 46844-2 $2.75
- ☐ #13 **BEAST AND THE HALLOWEEN HORROR**.. 40335-9 $2.75
- ☐ #14 **EMILY ARROW PROMISES TO DO BETTER THIS YEAR** 40369-3 $2.75
- ☐ #15 **MONSTER RABBIT RUNS AMUCK!** 40424-X $2.95

At your local bookstore or use this handy page for ordering:

DELL READERS SERVICE, DEPT. DPG
P.O. Box 5057, Des Plaines, IL. 60017-5057

Please send me the above title(s). I am enclosing $_____.
(Please add $2.50 per order to cover shipping and handling.) Send check or money order—no cash or C.O.D.s please.

Ms./Mrs./Mr. _____

Address _____

City/State _____ Zip _____

DPG-3/91

Prices and availability subject to change without notice. Please allow four to six weeks for delivery.